Just a Cowboy's Midnight Bride

Flyboys of Sweet Briar Ranch in North Dakota
Book Four
Jessie Gussman

Published By: Jessie Gussman

Contents

Acknowledgments

Cover art by Julia Gussman
Editing by Heather Hayden
Narration by Jay Dyess
Author Services by CE Author Assistant

Listen to a FREE professionally performed and produced audiobook version of this title on Youtube. Search for "Say With Jay" to browse all available FREE Dyess/Gussman audiobooks.

Chapter 1

Mav Stryker stumbled to the kitchen, rubbing his bleary eyes and groping for a coffee cup.

He needed caffeine to soothe the ache and the pounding in his head.

Unfortunately, in the dim glow of the light above the sink, he could see the cupboard was empty.

Rats.

He remembered using his last clean coffee cup two days ago, and yesterday he'd had to rinse one out.

He glanced at the sink. Overflowing with dirty dishes.

Doing dishes was something he hated. Along with cooking. And housework.

He needed a wife.

He'd already tried a maid. She'd quit after one week.

He'd tried a second one, but she must have talked to the first, because she never even showed up for the first day of work.

With one hand pressing against his temple where the throbbing was the worst, he padded to the sink, looking for a cup that would be the easiest to grab and wash.

Both sides of the sink were full to overflowing, so running water over anything would be tricky. But he needed coffee.

Not only for the pounding in his head, but he needed the jolt to jump-start his brain, to check his bank statement, to see that what he had been tossing and turning about all night was not just a bad dream.

Surely it was a bad dream.

The old linoleum on the floor peeled up, and he stumbled as he brought the semi-clean coffee cup to his one-cup dispenser, put it under the drip, and pressed the button to start. He leaned against the chipped, cheap countertop and pulled his phone out of his pajama pocket.

While the coffee dripped, he tried to focus his bleary eyes on his bank app.

Unfortunately, it took less than a minute for him to realize that he had not imagined it. He was almost broke.

The venture he'd invested all of his capital in—crossbreeding Highlander cattle with Herefords—had not panned out the way he had thought it was going to.

He'd overextended his capital and overestimated the profits while underestimating expenses. He hadn't expected last winter to be quite as bad as what it was. Winter in North Dakota was always bad, but it had been an exceptionally hard year, and he'd had to buy more hay than he planned on.

With the fact that he was already upside down, it had left him with next to nothing.

Last month, the mortgage on the farm had pretty much drained him, and then an unexpected illness in his herd, and the subsequent vet bills, had completely wiped him out.

He didn't know what he was going to do.

Maybe dishes and housework weren't the only things he needed a wife for.

He could just hear his sister Lark saying "no wonder you're not married when that's what you think a wife is for." But wasn't that what a wife was supposed to do? Keep the house?

He'd mulled over the biblical commands for a wife and couldn't come to any other conclusion. The woman was supposed to keep the house. That meant doing the dishes, doing the cleaning, and maybe, if he got a really good one, she'd fix some of the stuff that was broken around here, too.

Not that he wouldn't; he just hadn't had time. He'd been working so hard, had sunk everything that he'd made working every job he'd had for more than ten years into buying this spread. Then, he had a tip from an industry insider who'd said Highlander crosses were the next big thing. And when he researched it, the dude had been right. They'd been selling for triple the amount of good Angus beef.

Unfortunately, that must have just been a fluke in the market at the time that he'd researched, because the numbers hadn't held. He'd been waiting, hoping they would go back up, but last spring's calves were ready for market and he wasn't going to get nearly the price he expected for them.

His coffee was done, and he reached around, grabbing it, wincing at the heat, but drinking anyway.

It wasn't going to help him go back to sleep, but it would take his headache away.

His brothers all had money; even Lark, as a vet, would have money he could most likely borrow.

If he understood her correctly, someone had paid for her eight years of schooling, and she had no student debt.

He supposed, as one of her brothers, he should have found out exactly who paid for that school, but the idea hadn't occurred to him until just now, and he dismissed it. He didn't have time to think about that.

He needed to figure out a solution to his problem. And it didn't include going to his brothers. He wasn't going to lose face with them. They already thought he was the flighty one. The one that didn't have a head on his shoulders. No brain. And to a certain extent, they were right.

Maybe part of him not being good with women was because what his brothers thought was somewhat true. That and he was always focused on himself and what the woman he was with could do for him.

That was something Lark had told him once upon a time, and he dismissed it as ridiculous. Now, with his track record bearing witness that there was some kind of issue with him, he probably should give it more credence.

But the most pressing issue was figuring out what to do without telling his brothers. He didn't want them to think he was a failure. Any more than they already did. He was the flighty one. The one who never stuck with anything. Always goofing off. Couldn't concentrate without being distracted by the next shiny thing.

The Hereford-Highlander cross was probably just another in his long string of things that he had gotten distracted with and hadn't worked out.

That's what his brothers would say; he could hear them now.

Of course they would help him. They wouldn't want to see one of their family members lose their farm. They would make fun of him while they did it, though.

He winced again at the bitter brew, slightly less acidic this time than last but still burning his throat as he swallowed.

There had to be a solution.

Why don't you pray?

He believed in God. He would even say he loved God. He was saved for sure, but the God stuff had always seemed a little boring to him.

He hadn't always wanted to do things God's way because he was afraid he might miss something. Might miss out on something fun, or God might tell him to do something like go be a missionary in Africa, which was the very last thing he ever wanted to do.

He'd wanted to have a farm, wanted it to be successful, and he didn't want to spout preacher-ish nonsense to people who weren't interested in hearing it.

To people who were going to hell without someone to tell them the Way.

That little voice in his head seemed to be getting louder and louder. Then of course, it was always right.

Fine. I'll do whatever You want me to do, God, if You just save me from this mess I'm in right now.

He'd made similar promises over the years; a couple of times when he'd been in actual physical danger, he'd prayed that God would save him. After all, he felt like he was too young to die. And he'd said that he would serve God for the rest of his life if God would just get him out of that mess.

He hadn't exactly kept those promises. It wouldn't surprise him at all if God decided to give up on him and not listen to him or help him again.

I'm serious this time. If You help me out of this mess, I'll get serious about reading my Bible. I'll pray. And...

Could he say it? Could he really tell God he would give his life in service to the Lord?

What if God wanted him to become a preacher?

His older brother, Clay, carried the nickname Preacher, not because he was one, but because he had been wise from his youth up.

Mav certainly didn't have any such nickname.

Part of him wished he had. Part of him wanted to be that wise and thoughtful person that everyone went to for advice.

Part of him didn't want to be that boring.

But if he didn't do something, he was going to lose the ranch, and from where he could see, there was no human solution in sight.

He could sell all of his cows, and that would take care of his outstanding bills, but it wouldn't pay his mortgage for the rest of the year, and he would have no income in order to do that. His payment was way too high for him to get a regular job that would do anything more than supplement what he had.

Unless he got a job that paid six figures a year.

That was highly unlikely. All he knew was ranching, a little bit of rodeo, and he'd done ice road trucking in Alaska. But a truck-driving job wouldn't help. After all, it would only supplement his income, but it would take him away from the ranch and keep him from being able to farm full time.

Lord... I will try as hard as I am capable of to live my life for You. I...haven't always been very dependable, and that's probably not going to change overnight, but...I'm willing. I know that's not much, and I don't blame You if You don't do anything, but...it's all I have. You can have me if You want me, Lord. But I wouldn't blame You if You don't. There's not much of worth here.

He didn't admit that to just anyone. In fact, he wouldn't admit it to anyone, other than the Lord.

God didn't need him to admit it. God already knew that a lot of his bluster was just for show. Because he was insecure and felt inferior. After all, all of his brothers were successful. Successful in life, success in farming, successful in their marriages. And here he was, successful at nothing. Not life, not farming—he thought again of his empty bank account—and definitely not in relationships.

Basically, he was a failure, and what in the world would God want to have to do with a failure?

Chapter 2

Go look at your bills again.

The feeling was so strong, Mav almost looked over his shoulder to see if the words had been spoken aloud.

He'd already looked at his bills for three hours last night. And he'd looked at them every evening for the last month. There wasn't anything new there.

Go. Look.

Sighing, he walked over to the small table that doubled as his desk. It had one drawer in the front, and he had a little plastic thing with shelves set on it on one side.

His small attempt at organization.

He might as well have not bothered, since the desk was littered with letters and bills and invoices and bank statements. Receipts, bills of sale, and a few pieces of junk mail that he'd never gotten around to throwing away. His garbage can overflowed, and he hadn't taken the time to empty that, any more than he'd taken the time to do his dishes or sweep the dirt off his floor.

He looked at the desk, knowing that he'd gone through every single thing at least a dozen times in the last two weeks.

Open the drawer.

He didn't typically use the drawer. It was just for stuff that he wanted to save and didn't have the time to go through at the moment. Not bills, but other things.

He stood staring at the drawer. Why would he open it?

Just do it.

Humor lit his face, although he didn't quite smile. He wasn't sure where the voice in his head was coming from, but wasn't that what faith was? Just doing something he knew he should, even though he couldn't see where it would have any conceivable effect on any part of his life.

He didn't smile, but he did reach his hand out and opened the drawer.

It was stuffed with envelopes, most of them opened, though some of them not. The drawer was stuffed so full that he had to tug, then use his other hand to flatten some of the envelopes to get it open.

When was the last time he'd gone through any of this stuff?

Christmas cards that he'd stuffed in there, thinking that he would get the address and send one back to the sender, made up the bulk of the items.

Letters of inquiry from back when he was working the ice roads. A few letters from the national bull riders association. It hadn't taken him but a season or two of that to decide that breaking his body over an animal for the entertainment of crazy people who seemed to enjoy that type of thing was not his cup of tea.

He could see how it would be addicting to some men. He loved the adrenaline rush and, honestly, loved the attention, but hadn't loved the way his body felt while he was doing it.

The idea of being successful because of luck of the draw was something that appealed to him on a surface level, but internally he revolted against that type of win. Using the word "win" loosely.

Figuring he might as well clear out the drawer, throwing out any of the bull riding letters as well as the ice road trucking letters, he grabbed a big handful and drew the mass out of the drawer.

Maybe he shouldn't throw the stuff away. If he lost his farm, he'd need a job. He was semi-decent at both of those things, although he'd been better at the trucking than the bull riding.

But as he thought that, his eyes landed on a letter that had been exposed when he pulled the top layer away.

He didn't remember that one. There was a lawyer firm address in the upper left-hand corner, with his address written in neat handwriting, which was odd since lawyers' offices usually typed things up.

He knew that much from buying his ranch.

Carefully, he set the big pile of envelopes in his hand down and picked up the letter that caught his eye.

Peregrine Czeitzler, Attorney at Law.

Hmm. That name didn't ring any bells for him. And if he was thinking correctly, that town under the name wasn't around here but almost two hours away.

Why would he have a letter from a law office he didn't know anything about? It wasn't opened, so he broke the seal and ran his thumb along the end, opening the top of the envelope, and pulled out one typed page on a thin, cheap piece of paper.

His eyes skimmed over it, and then he read it more slowly.

Dear Mr. Maverick Stryker,

This letter is to inform you that you have been chosen by an anonymous benefactor to receive the sum of one billion ($1,000,000,000) dollars upon the event of your successful marriage.

There are some stipulations, of course, and those are:

1. You must stay married for at least a year, or you will return the amount of money that you have been given after taxes.

2. You must stay in North Dakota. Your bride must stay in North Dakota, too.

The purpose of these stipulations is to keep people who have grown up in North Dakota from leaving our great state, and the purpose of the money is to have you invest back in your state, becoming successful and prosperous in North Dakota, hopefully attracting other businesses and good people to our beautiful state.

There have been other people who have been given this letter and given a time frame in which to marry. You are a bit more of a wildcard, so this is not a blind letter sent to everyone, but something that has been tailored to fit your needs.

Therefore, you have until—

Mav read the date, read it again, and then grabbed his phone and looked at it.

The date was today. He had until today at midnight to get married, and he could inherit one billion dollars!

He almost threw his phone down and ran back to his bedroom to get dressed, but it was two o'clock in the morning, and he wasn't going to do anything right now.

At six o'clock, he could go to the diner, and then...do what?

Hold a sign up in front of him that said "Marry Me?"

And the idea that there was so much money involved... Even though he wanted the money, wanted to get married, it rankled him to think that he would have some woman marrying him just because they were going to inherit one billion dollars. If someone was going to marry him, he wanted it to be because of him, not because of his money. Not that this was even his money yet, but the idea that she needed to look at him and see him, and not see one billion dollars, somehow got stuck in his brain and seemed like the most important thing.

He wanted a woman who was willing to drop everything and marry him.

Was there such a woman?

He read the letter again, checking the date twice more before he slowly sank into his desk chair.

There weren't too many times in his life where he was slow, or where he wasn't moving, but this was one of those times where he had been shocked into immobility.

He told himself not to be silly. He would take whatever woman would have him, and if the money was a draw, then the money was a draw.

But a different, and maybe more mature, part of him said that if he didn't get the money, it might be better than to end up married to someone who couldn't stand him but who was going to try to put up with him for one billion dollars.

He tapped the letter with his finger, warring with himself. But he was pretty sure about this. Losing the farm would be terrible, and the last thing he wanted to do, but being married, stuck for the rest of his life with a woman who didn't want him, would be worse.

And if they ever got divorced, he'd have to pay all the money back. That would be worse than losing the farm.

Feeling like maybe this was the first mature decision he'd ever made in his life, he decided that in his mind.

And then he remembered his promise.

Sorry, Lord. I got a little excited over the one billion. But this was obviously an answer to prayer. There's no other way to explain it. I don't remember putting this letter here, and this is a crazy thing to have happen.

Was it even legit?

His mom had married businessman Howard Edwards, and he would probably know or have the contacts to find out in less time than Mav anyway.

Of course, Mav could drive to the lawyer's office to find out, but if it was legit, he didn't want to waste any time.

So, therefore, he would drive to his mom's house, not first thing, because Howard wouldn't be able to get any of his contacts up until nine o'clock, probably, so by nine. He'd drive there by nine.

And in the meantime, he would finish praying—this had to be a God thing, there was just no other explanation for it—and then he'd make a list of all the girls in Sweet Water who were of marriageable age.

Of course, all he had to do was actually tell a couple of ladies in town that he was looking for a wife and wanted to marry her by midnight, and the news would go around town like wildfire. If there was anyone who was actually interested in marrying him, he would hear sooner rather than later.

Small towns were good for something anyway.

With that thought in mind, he decided that his regular prayer position of sitting in his chair was not going to cut it, and he got down on his knees, bending his face forward until his forehead touched the floor.

Lord, I was serious about my life. It's worthless. Worthless without You. I want to become the man that You want me to be, to be Your servant, living for You. I want everything I do to be less about Mav Stryker and all about giving You glory.

Right there, that was a bold prayer and unlike anything he'd ever prayed before. He paused, because while he meant it with all his heart, he wasn't sure he could actually do it.

I'm probably going to mess up, Lord. I guess You already know that.

He talked to the Lord just a little more, or maybe it was a lot, because his knees and legs were stiff when he rose from the floor, and his coffee was cold when he took a big sip. He shuddered but swallowed it anyway. His headache was gone, and his mind felt clear for the first time in a very long time. Confident that he would have a bride by dinnertime—after all, this was all being orchestrated by a Power much higher than himself—he started to make the list.

Chapter 3

Cassie walked down the sidewalk of Sweet Water, her head down, lost in thought. Miss June had been diagnosed with cancer and was facing surgery soon. Cassie had just delivered a casserole to the community center for Miss June to take home and heat up for supper.

Miss June hadn't seemed any worse than she usually was. Cassie didn't know what she was expecting to see when she saw her for the first time since her diagnosis, but it wasn't a woman who was smiling serenely, calmly crafting like she didn't have some kind of dread disease growing and reproducing inside of her own body.

She knew what it was like to have the dreaded word cancer given to her in a cold and impersonal doctor's office.

It stunk.

But maybe that's what age did to a person. Age and a solid foundation in knowing God. After all, if one knew God and had grown to trust Him over years of daily time with Him, then she supposed it would only be natural to trust in Him when a diagnosis like that hit.

It made Cassie want to redouble her efforts to have a consistent time with the Lord.

She planned it, but the plan wasn't always executed as sometimes her days got busy as her workload increased or as other plans morphed and took over.

It was the one thing she knew she should protect, because if she ever faced such a diagnosis again, she wanted to handle it just as well as Miss June had.

She planned on going home, and was headed in that direction, when something nudged her elbow, and she turned around, startled.

"Hey, Billy," she said, staring at the large, hairy face of the Highlander steer that roamed Sweet Water freely.

The cow nudged her again.

His horns spread out and up, and the cow seemed to be careful not to hit her with them as he pushed his nose against her.

"Do you want to be petted?" she asked, surprised that the cow was giving her the time of day.

From what she had seen, he spent most of his days chasing the pig the townsfolk had dubbed Munchy that also wandered around in Sweet Water.

Regardless, Billy didn't seem to be interested in anything but nudging her, and after glancing around, she saw the pig wasn't anywhere in sight.

She patted Billy's head, and he shook it back and forth, moving her hand over the top of his head, making sure she got all of his itchy spots. But that didn't seem to calm him, and he nudged her again, pushing her a little bit, and she stumbled back.

"What do you want?"

He looked up at her with soulful eyes.

"Are you hungry?" That was the only thing she could think of that could be wrong with him. The needs of a bovine were pretty basic. Unless he wanted her to go find Munchy for him.

"I don't have any food. I don't usually feed cows. I just have dog food at home."

He gave her another nudge with his nose, and she looked around as she caught her balance, noticing the feed store was just two stores down.

"You really want me to go get you something to eat?" she asked, wondering if cows were that smart. Did he really know where the feed store was? Was he really pushing her toward it?

She didn't really have much experience with cows, and she most likely never would.

After all, the man she'd been crushing on her entire life owned a ranch, but he'd never given her the time of day, and that wasn't likely to change.

She'd mostly come to grips with it, come to grips with the idea that she would do whatever God wanted her to do and whatever He put in her path. She would try to be content.

She wasn't exactly sure she was going to be able to do that, but to the best of her ability, that's what she had decided. After all, she wasn't going to chase some guy around and demand that he pay attention to her or even like her. It just wasn't going to happen. She had a little bit more pride than that.

Plus, Mav Stryker, the object of her crush, definitely wasn't interested in a girl like her, someone who was quiet and retiring. A little shy even. Someone who was known as "that girl who had cancer."

He lived an adventurous life, and he would want a girl who could match him stride for stride, do what he did, be ready to go on death-defying trips at the drop of a hat.

And that definitely wasn't her.

She'd looked at death very closely, did not like what she saw, and would prefer not to see it again for another eighty years or so.

Regardless, thinking about cows always made her think about Mav, but she shook that all from her mind. She'd given that up—Mav and her crush on him—to the Lord a year ago, and although once in a while, she was tempted to take that back up and deal with it on her own, she just had to trust God that He knew what He was doing when He was directing her life.

"All right. If you're hungry, I have some money I was putting back to buy a couple of books at the bookstore, but I can spend it on cow feed instead." She patted Billy a little bit more, then walked slowly toward the feed store, with him striding right by her side.

Funny, because Billy had never showed the slightest bit of interest in her.

When she got to the feed store, Billy nudged her. Well, maybe it was a little more than a nudge, since he caused her to stumble toward the door.

"I was going to the feed store. I told you that." She looked at him, a little annoyed, because he'd almost knocked her down. But if she had any doubt about where he wanted her to go, that doubt had been eradicated.

She had been planning on going home and spending the rest of the day cocooned in her office, working on a big project that she'd won a bid for and needed to have finished by the end of the week. But before she went, she could make a detour to the feed store and buy the cow some food.

"I don't usually feed you, but whoever does must have dropped the ball. I'm going to have to have a word with someone." She looked at Billy, nodding her head, thinking she would be doing him a favor.

Although, as she looked at him, it was hard to tell with all of that hair he had, but she still didn't think that he was missing too many meals.

Maybe the steer just wasn't going to be content until he had everyone in the town under his spell, buying him treats, petting him, and making detours out of their day to go to the feed store and get him his favorite treats.

The bell overhead jingled as she walked in, glancing once more over her shoulder at the cow who waited patiently on the sidewalk, his tail swishing, his head slightly down, his eyes lowering like he was going to take a nap while he was waiting for her.

He almost had human characteristics. He was so odd. Of course, she really didn't know much about cows, and she was almost certainly being fanciful about it.

The animal was motivated by his stomach, and his stomach was saying get food. And somehow, he'd figured out the people who came out of the store fed him.

That's all she could figure.

"Cassie. We don't usually get to see you around in here," Mr. Tate said from behind the counter.

Three other men stood in front of the counter, two of them leaning against it, one of them with his hands in his pockets and head tilted back, and she almost got the feeling that she was interrupting their conversation.

"I don't know if I've ever been in here more than two or three times," she said. She usually got her dog food and birdseed from here, but they delivered it for no charge since she lived in town.

She nodded at the other men that were standing there, recognizing Deuce, her friend Teagan's husband, and also Clay "Preacher" Stryker, who wasn't in town very often and was a good bit older than Cassie, but she knew him from church and highly respected him.

The third man she thought was one of the men who had bought the Sweet Briar Ranch north of town. She thought his name was Gideon, but she wasn't exactly sure. Still, she nodded at all of them as they greeted her with a couple of comments about the weather.

"What brings you here today? Are we late on our dog food delivery?" Mr. Tate said, reaching as though he was going to turn to the computer and look her up.

"No. Phyllis doesn't eat much, and you guys keep her stocked up really well in treats and food."

"Then you ran out of birdseed?" Mr. Tate said, clicking a few keys on the computer.

"No. I'm good on the birdseed too." She gave a weak laugh, a little embarrassed. "I... I was hoping I could get some cow feed, or treats, or something. Billy seems hungry today."

"Billy seems hungry?" Gideon asked, his eyes lifting in a bit of disbelief.

"I can't imagine that old bovine would be hungry. Not with the way everyone is constantly feeding him around here. It's amazing that he doesn't weigh two thousand pounds," Preacher, his voice languid, his posture straight, commented with the barest hint of a grin.

"I'll say. Teagan loves that thing. In fact, she'd like to take him home. She just can't catch him."

"I haven't really petted him until today. He came over, pushed his nose against me a bunch of times, and almost knocked me down to try to get me to come in here. I assumed he was hungry and figured I would grab him something to eat before I went home and started working."

"Are you trying to tell us that the steer directed you to come in here?" Deuce said, and if it had been anybody else, she might have been offended at the humor in his tone.

"I know it sounds crazy, but that's exactly what I'm saying. I'm not lying. That's what he did."

"I think I've heard everything today—a cow that leads people to the feed store and a man who thinks he's going to announce to the town that he's getting married and expects to have a bride step forward—no offense to your brother," Mr. Tate said, looking at Preacher as he said that last bit.

Normally Cassie wouldn't have paid any attention to the rumors that were going around town, but it was Mr. Tate's glance at Preacher that perked up her ears. Preacher was Mav's brother.

"Someone's getting married today?" she asked, picking up on a little bit of what they said and deliberately misunderstanding, hoping someone would fill in the gaps for her. Preacher only had one brother who wasn't married that she knew of.

Preacher, who was almost always extremely stoic, looked a little bit uncomfortable and shifted where he stood, shoving his hands into his pockets.

But it was Deuce that answered.

"Mav Stryker announced this morning that he would be getting married today and invited anyone who wanted to to step into the church with him, and they'd do the deed."

Cassie felt like her stomach hit her feet and exploded.

Chapter 4

"Who's he getting married to?" Cassie asked, imagining that girls would be lined up for blocks for the opportunity.

She would be. Except, she wouldn't want him to be stuck with her.

She might have a crush on him, and had for a long time, but he had zero interest in her.

She matured a little in the last year, and she realized that part of love was letting go. Or not burdening someone that you love with the need to make you happy.

In this case, the case of Mav, she knew her affection would always be one-sided, and she didn't want to make him feel guilty or bad because he couldn't return her feelings.

Still, while she had given it to God and pretty much reconciled herself to the fact that he would not be marrying her, the idea of him marrying someone else felt painful in a way she could barely describe. It made it hard to keep her breathing steady and made it feel like there were ice shards in her chest.

Her heart flopped like a dying fish, and she wasn't quite sure how she managed to keep her feet under her and her knees from buckling.

"Well, he hasn't yet. He surely thought there was going to be a long line of ladies who wanted the honor, but no one has stepped forward. He wants to do it tonight." Gideon glanced at Preacher as he said that, almost as though he didn't want to offend the man.

But from what Cassie had always heard and observed, Preacher was unoffendable.

"Have you talked to him?" Deuce asked, directing his question at Preacher.

Preacher held his hands out. "In here with you all is the first I heard about it." He shrugged his shoulders. "I suppose I'll try, but I haven't had a chance yet."

"Well, he announced it as he was going through town. Apparently he was headed out to talk to your mother. Something about needing some advice from her husband."

Preacher lifted his chin but didn't say anything to that. Cassie almost scratched her head, because Mrs. Stryker had married a businessman. Why would Mav, a rancher, need his advice? She knew ranching was like a business, but the things that ranchers typically talked about were cattle and diseases, the market and the weather. Not the business side.

She decided to speak up. "You guys know more than the ladies at the community center. I just came back from delivering a casserole to Miss June, and they never mentioned any of this." She wished she wouldn't have heard it. Now...she wanted to check in on Mav. If there really wasn't a bunch of ladies waiting in line, maybe she would have a chance.

But then she remembered her vow. She would let God bring him to her. She wasn't going to go chasing after him, beating off a bunch of other women to try to be first in line. She couldn't imagine that was what the Lord wanted her to do. Not after the years she'd spent trying to get her mind off its infatuation with him.

Definitely there were a lot of things to think about, and she was whirling them all over in her brain when Mr. Tate interrupted her musings. "I can get you just a small amount, enough for you to feed him one time. Is that what you're thinking?"

It took her a minute, then she nodded her head and tried not to be obvious about the fact that the conversation had left her reeling.

"That's fine. Exactly what I was thinking. Something that you know he likes, his favorite, if possible."

"Sounds like someone has you wrapped around his little...hoof," Deuce said with a grin.

"Or horn. They're kind of wicked looking."

"He didn't hurt you, did he?" Preacher asked, concern in his tone. A lot of people treated her like she was made of glass, since she had cancer.

Preacher, on the other hand, treated everyone with respect and consideration.

Just the right amount. No one ever thought he was being too flirty or inappropriate.

She looked at him more like a father figure, even though he wasn't quite old enough to be her dad.

He settled a hand on her shoulder, looking into her eyes.

"No. He was a perfect gentleman. Even being careful to move his head so his horns didn't catch me. I think he's just hungry."

"As long as you're sure you're okay." Clay's eyes were serious. "He's been known to chase a few people. And there was a rumor about him putting a hole in someone's T-shirt. If he's a danger to society, we'll have to be serious about rounding him up, as much as Sweet Water seems to love her unofficial mascot." He said the last part with a little bit of a grin, and that made her smile.

It was true. Sweet Water loved that they had a Highlander cow and pig that roamed freely around town.

She wouldn't want to be the cause of having either of them rounded up, but she knew she could be honest when she said, "No. Really. He's been perfectly behaved. I even think he was being a little bit protective of me."

"Here you go. And you don't owe anything. There's actually a fund that's been set up here. Various people have put money down on it, to provide food for him whenever he needs it. I'll just take that out of the fund and won't charge you."

"Oh. I didn't know that."

"It is not something I advertise. Because I wouldn't want anyone to take advantage of it, but I know you're not going to. And the money's there, so we might as well use it."

She nodded, taking the small amount of feed he put in a bag, then watching as he picked up a smaller bag.

"These are treats. He's liked them before, but sometimes he turns his nose up at them. I think it just depends on what mood he's in."

"He's moody like a mare?" Deuce said, and the men laughed.

Cassie smiled, because she'd overheard people talking about how mares could be moody at church on occasion, but she never actually experienced it for herself. Riding horses and dealing with cattle was probably not something she would ever do. Even if she kind of wanted to.

"Thank you so much. I appreciate it."

"You probably know this, but there's a place to feed him behind the diner. There's an empty lot back there, and there are a couple of pans set out. I think Jane usually makes sure that his water is filled up on a daily basis, and there's a little spot for the pig too." Mr. Tate smiled. "Here's a small bag for it."

She took the third bag, thanking him again. "Are you sure I don't owe you anything?"

"No. I would tell you if the fund wasn't enough, but there's plenty of money there. The town of Sweet Water takes care of him pretty well."

"He's a sweetheart. I can see why they do."

She nodded at the men again, pleased that she'd been able to act so normal when her insides felt like they were melting. And her heart, goodness, she didn't even know what to say about her heart. It hurt. For real. And yet, there was nothing she could do.

Mav was going to get married today, and that would be the end of that.

Maybe the Lord had convicted her to get her mind off of him and focus on living her life for Him, just so this would hurt less than it would have if she would have still had her crush on him.

She couldn't even imagine how she would have reacted if she would have found this out last year this time, before she'd given the idea of having Mav for herself to the Lord. She told God that she was willing to do whatever He wanted, to marry whomever He brought in, or stay single if that was His plan for her, and she wouldn't pine after a man who wasn't interested in her.

It hadn't been an easy decision, and she had relapsed plenty of times, but she was determined to get him out of her mind or at least put him in a spot where he belonged. Not on a pedestal where she always had him.

Ugh. Still, this was a hard blow.

The bell jingled again as she walked out. Billy stood on the sidewalk where she'd left him.

He didn't act overly hungry, though, as she opened the bag of treats, putting one in her hand and holding it out, hoping he didn't take her hand along with the treat.

But he barely sniffed at it, shaking his head a little and turning his head away.

"You're kidding. You pushed me into the feed store, and now you're not even going to eat your treats? You're going to make me look like an idiot. I told those men you were hungry."

Her light reprimand did nothing to persuade the bovine to eat what she offered, and finally she shook her head, put the treat back in the bag, and started walking toward the diner. She would put this stuff in his feeding trough, and if he ate it right away, great. If he didn't, it would be there for when he was hungry.

Billy didn't follow her across the street and back toward the feeding trough.

Carefully putting the feed in and the treats on top and then putting the pig feed in its bowl, she tried to tell herself that God was in control. That she needed to trust and have faith that He was going to work everything out for her good and His glory. That she didn't have to go running in, trying to push herself into a position where Mav might possibly be hers.

There were plenty of other girls who would want him and be better for him, and she'd already accepted that.

This was just a red herring, something the devil was dangling in front of her trying to get her off the track of following God and doing only His will.

She'd almost convinced herself of that by the time she'd emptied the feed into the bowls and turned around to walk home.

Chapter 5

"He's here," Bonnie said, looking over her shoulder at her husband. She couldn't keep the worry out of her eyes and knew there were lines in her forehead, knew her hand clutched the curtain too tightly.

"It's okay, Bonnie," he said, coming over and putting a hand on either side of her arms, pulling her back into his chest. His hands were light on her arms, but warmth seeped through his fingers, calming her.

She leaned back into him, relishing the warmth and strength that she could feel oozing out of him. So many years, she had been a mother alone, and it felt so good to be able to lean on someone. Not expect them to do life for her, but to know that they shared her burden, her love for her children, and her desire to see them turn out right.

"That's why we gave him extra time in the letter. To give him time to grow up."

"But if he's here because of the letter, that means he just found it, which means that he really hasn't grown up because it would have just been chance that he would have gone through whatever pile of stuff he threw it in."

She had been so sure that he had thrown it away. Worried that he had. Knowing that financial difficulties were slowly strangling him as she watched the joy fade out of his eyes in recent weeks and months.

"God has this. It's in His plan. If it's meant to be, he would have found it. If it's not, he wouldn't have. It's that simple."

"Do you think he's here to ask to borrow money?" she asked, not wanting the answer to be affirmative. She didn't know what she'd do.

She wanted her children to learn to work, to support themselves and make a positive contribution to society, and they had. They hadn't had much choice when they were younger, since it had been a struggle to survive.

Ever since her marriage to Howard, she had more money than she knew what to do with, not that she spent a lot. She'd bought herself a couple things that she'd wanted all of her life—landscaping around her house and a Friesian horse. Those had been her only two expenditures, and they hadn't even been a total of ten grand.

Considering her husband was worth billions, and she could have anything she wanted, it was kinda frugal. But she was content and knew that money didn't make a person happy.

Mav did not know how filthy rich Howard and she were. But he would know if they had anything extra, they wouldn't want to see him go without.

Although, failing, whether it was bankruptcy, or in a business venture, or even a marriage, there were lessons to be learned, lessons that a person couldn't learn if someone bailed them out.

"We'll cross that bridge when we come to it. We'll definitely pray about it and not make any rash decisions. After all, we want what God wants for him, not what we want."

She nodded against his chest, feeling so safe and reassured that he felt the same way she did, and secure in the knowledge that he would guide them in the way that God wanted them to go. At least to the best of his ability, since Howard was just a man and prone to making mistakes the same way any man was.

She could forgive any mistake he made, knowing that he would make it sincerely, trying to do the best he could, and she wouldn't expect him to be perfect.

"It's going to be okay, Bonnie. I promise. And you know it too, because God's going to make sure that everything works out for the best for Mav."

"I just want him to find someone. For him to find God first, but for him to find a woman who loves him for what he is. And not for the bluster that he puts on."

"I know God has someone in mind for him. It's just a matter of him being ready for her. After all, you don't want her to walk into a marriage with him when he's not ready to treat her the way she needs to be treated."

"No. Of course not. I love her, and I don't even know who she is. I want her to be treated right. I would be so ashamed if one of my boys didn't treat his wife like the precious gift she is."

"That's exactly how I would describe you. Precious gift. I hope you know that." He bent down, kissing her neck below her ear and moving to the sensitive spot that he knew that she loved while one of his hands lifted and rubbed across the back of her neck, giving her shivers. She loved it, that light touch that made her feel so loved and cherished.

He knew it, and she wouldn't say he used it to his advantage, but he definitely used it to let her know that he loved her.

She said a quick prayer, asking the Lord to help her keep her mouth shut and not say anything that she shouldn't say, to allow Mav a chance to say whatever it was he needed to say. She didn't want to tell him about the letter if that wasn't what he was there for. She and Howard had agreed that if he had thrown it away, it was his loss. As tempted as she had been over the years to mention it.

There was a perfunctory knock on the door before it opened, and Mav strode in.

Immediately she noticed a difference in his demeanor. Maybe it was because she was his mother and knew him so well, or maybe she was looking for, praying for, hoping that he would find the letter and that it wouldn't ruin him.

Money ruined so many people, but so far, all of her children had handled it well.

"Good morning, Mom," Mav said, nodding his head at both of them.

"Good morning, son. Would you like a cup of coffee? Or some eggs?"

"No thanks. I've already had six cups today." He lifted a shoulder in a shrug, and one side of his lips turned up, but the carefree look that she'd loved so much in her youngest and most irresponsible son was just a shadow of what it usually was.

"I'm actually here to ask Howard a business question. But..." He looked down, almost as though he were trying to figure out how to say what needed to be said.

He wasn't carrying any letter, didn't have anything but his phone tucked in his pocket, and she said another short prayer to heaven that she would be able to not say anything about the letter if he didn't say something first.

She didn't want to manipulate God's will. And while there might be times where people needed a reminder, she knew this wasn't one of them.

"Go ahead, son," Howard said gently. "We're listening."

Howard picked up on the same thing as she had. There was something going on, and Mav was going to say something...probably something unexpected.

She pressed imperceptibly closer to her husband and said another short prayer for her son. She loved him so much. Wanted him to be serious about his life and not keep wasting it.

"I had a little talk with the Lord this morning," he finally said, looking back up.

"That's good. I usually talk to Him every morning as well," she said softly, when he paused.

He gave her a baleful look. "I know you do. But it's not something I placed a priority on. But this morning, I guess I was driven to desperation, and I decided that was going to change."

She knew there had been something different. Knew he had looked different than normal. And she couldn't keep the smile from spreading across her face.

"I wasn't going to say anything to you, because I don't want you to get your hopes up. I doubt I'm going to all of a sudden be the perfect son that you've never had."

"You've been perfect to me. I've never complained. I love you with all my heart."

"I know. I know." He took a breath, but before he could say anything more, Howard said, "Would you like to sit down?"

He laughed. "You know me. I can't sit still. Actually, it would feel better if I were pacing, but it drives people nuts when I talk to them and pace at the same time, so I was trying to be considerate."

Bonnie turned her head to look at Howard, and they shared a smile. That was so true.

"I haven't been serious about my walk with the Lord. Not like I should have been. I've found myself in a financial mess."

Bonnie's heart dropped.

He put a hand up. "I'm not asking you for money. Couldn't do that. I would lose the farm first. That's what I was thinking this morning."

Her heart went out to him, but she was proud of him as well. She wanted him to stand on his own two feet, if he could. Men were to care for women, and they weren't to go back to their parents unless there was a dire need. A sickness, perhaps. Cancer, or an illness in one of his children. Go back to care for his parents in their old age. But not because he made foolish decisions in his business.

"Anyway, I suppose that's what drove me to my knees, truly." He looked like he steeled himself but didn't look embarrassed to be kneeling in front of his creator. Of course not.

"For some reason, I was prompted to open a drawer in my desk. One I hadn't opened for quite some time. Years even. Other than to stuff things in it. I took out a pile, intending to go through them, and I found a letter. It...came from a law firm that I'm not sure is legit. I'm here because I thought maybe Howard could scope it out, using some of his contacts, and let me know if it's actually a law firm or if the letter is probably just a hoax."

Howard's hand, which now rested on her shoulder, squeezed gently.

She wanted to put her hand over top of it, rub her cheek against it, turning to kiss him, but she did none of those things.

Her children weren't supposed to know where the money came from. She did not want to be the weak link, the one to let the cat out of the bag, because up until this point, it had remained a mystery.

"I could probably look it up, call a few people if you want me to. What's the name of it?" Howard said casually, like he didn't know exactly what the letter said, exactly where it came from, and exactly how legitimate it was.

And exactly how much time Mav had left to fill the conditions of the letter.

Bonnie closed her eyes. Less than eighteen hours. Fifteen was more like it.

She reminded herself that God was in control and her worry did nothing to solve any problems. She tried to picture in her mind just letting go and saying *God, I trust You. Please work this out.*

"That's what I was hoping you would offer. I have a picture of the letter, so I wasn't hauling it around Sweet Water with me, accidentally misplacing it or something," Mav said, pulling out his phone.

So that's why he wasn't carrying a letter. Bonnie tried not to smile. She didn't want him to know how relieved she was. That almost seemed like a mature decision on his part, and she was proud of him. Sometimes it was just a matter of knowing a person's weakness and compensating for that. After all, no one was perfect, and everyone had weaknesses.

She didn't say anything as Mav held out his phone, and Howard glanced at it, reading the name of the law firm and then nodding.

"I've heard of this one. I can't tell myself that it's legit, but I'll do a little bit of digging right now, if you don't mind waiting. Just to confirm what I already believe I know."

"I don't mind waiting at all. It's kind of important."

Howard hadn't looked at the phone long enough to read the letter, if he could even see it because of it being too small.

Mav didn't say anything else but stood, fidgeting and waiting.

As his mother, she knew he must be bursting at the seams to talk about it, but she was proud of him that he didn't. Didn't brag. That was definitely a new leaf, since Mav was almost always known as a braggart.

Maybe he wasn't going to tell anyone about it. Maybe he was really going to keep it to himself.

Or maybe just until he got the money.

Howard dialed the number, then turned his back and walked a few paces away, speaking low into the phone. Mav turned to her.

"The letter says that I'm going to inherit some money but I have to be married."

"Really?" she asked, trying to look interested and surprised, but not astounded. It sounded a little odd, and the fact that he was checking out the attorney from whence it came showed that he was being responsible. She didn't want to overreact and arouse his suspicions.

"I had the letter stuffed away. It came a while ago. I...really felt like it was the Lord showing it to me today, especially after the prayer I prayed and because the deadline for me to get married is tonight."

"Tonight?" she said, tilting her head and lifting her brows, giving him a mother's look.

"Yeah." His lips curved up in something very close to his normal devil-may-care smile. "I know that's pretty short notice."

"It is. Especially since, as far as I know, you don't have anyone lined up."

"I don't. But I did mention in town that I was planning on getting married by the end of the day and anyone who was interested should look me up."

"I see. And now your phone's ringing off the hook?" She raised her brows and looked down at his silent, dark phone.

"Not exactly." He looked a little embarrassed, abashed maybe. And again, her heart bled for him.

He had always found it hard to relate to women, mostly because he had a hard time being gentle, considerate, and unselfish.

It didn't take women long to see that while he might give lip service to politeness and manners, in reality, his concern was mostly for himself, and he wasn't really thinking about them. Not enough to put them first or ahead of himself.

Maybe that would have changed, or started changing, along with everything else this morning. She hoped so. For the sake of the woman he found to marry him, if he found one.

"Any advice for me on that end?" he asked after he seemed to hesitate.

"You mean if the letter is legit, you're actually considering marrying someone by the end of the day?" she asked, as though she wasn't as familiar as she was with the details of the letter.

"Yeah. It's a lot of money, Mom. I... I guess I don't really want to talk about that other than I think it would be worth it to get married."

"A lifetime of misery isn't worth all the money in the world. And that's what a marriage would be, unless you're not planning on staying married?"

"The letter says we have to. We have to stay married and live in North Dakota. I guess I know you're right. I know that being married to the wrong person is worse than not being married at all, no matter how much money is involved."

"That's absolutely true," she said firmly, knowing it was. She wasn't leading him wrong there. She was definitely guiding him in the right direction.

"But surely you remember what you always said. It is less important to be 'in love,'" he used air quotes around the words "in love," "than it is to have shared values and morals. And have a mutual respect. To be willing to put yourself last and be married to someone who feels the same. Someone who would always be putting the other person first."

"And you want someone who keeps their word. Someone you can trust. Someone who is going to raise your children to believe the way you do. To love the Lord and serve Him. Who isn't going to browbeat your kids or give them a semblance of religion without the relationship with an Almighty God. It's not about rules, and it's not just about pie-in-the-sky love, it's about submitting to God, because He's your Creator, and having a relationship with Him, because He loves you and wants one."

"I know. I need the reminder, I guess. More for myself than for anyone I'm looking for. I... I guess I have a reputation that maybe isn't the most steady."

"I can't believe if there's a significant amount of money involved that people aren't lining up."

"I didn't mention the money. I... I remembered what you said, and I felt like it would be better if someone chose me for myself." He hung his head. "Maybe that's a little bit of pride too. I didn't want it to be about money. I want to see if there's anyone who will do it for me. Just me."

"I love you, and I love that decision. That's probably one of the most mature things that you've ever done. I admire you. And whether you find a woman who will take you, or whether you don't, God blesses humility and people who do right even though it's hard."

Mav nodded as though agreeing that the words she said made sense.

Her mother's heart cried out to her God, begging Him to bless this new direction of Mav's life. She wanted to ask for the perfect woman for him to appear today, but she didn't.

She'd been praying for Mav, and for his future mate, for years. Decades. But it had to be in God's time. As much as she wanted Mav to be able to get the money and the woman, she doubted it would happen.

So she just prayed again, *Lord. Please, work Your will in his life. Whatever it takes to bring him to You, please.*

"Yes. This lawyer, Peregrine Czeitzler, Attorney at Law, is totally legit. He's a little bit eccentric, but sometimes those are the best people to work with. Because they work out of the box." Howard smiled, and Bonnie had no doubt he knew what he was talking about. He had worked out of the box a lot, although Mav wouldn't know that. Not the extent to which he had done it, anyway.

Howard didn't stop until he'd come back over to stand beside her, putting his arm around her, allowing her to lean into his strength if she chose to, which she did.

She'd spent so many years alone. So many years raising her children by herself as a single mom. It felt so good to have someone standing beside her. Of course she was going to lean into his strength and offer him hers and whatever else he needed, at any point.

Marriage was a two-way street, and she didn't want anyone to ever say that she didn't do more than her share. She loved Howard and wanted him to know it. Even if that meant sacrificing herself for him. She would gladly do it. Because that's what true love was. Forgoing oneself and putting the other person first. Not being selfish, or rude, or inconsiderate. But loving the way Jesus loved.

"Good to know. So, you would trust what the letter said?" Mav asked.

"Yes. Whatever it says, I would say you can take it to the bank." Howard lifted his lips a little as Bonnie looked around at him, and their eyes met.

She loved his sense of humor too. He always made her smile.

"All right. Well, wish me luck. I'm off to see if I can find someone who will marry me in the next..." Mav pulled his hand up and looked at his watch. "Fifteen hours."

"I hope you find the right woman," she said, wanting to say so much more but forcing herself to stop at that.

"If I have time, I'll bring her by for you to approve, Mom. Otherwise, I might just send you a text."

"All right."

She didn't say anything more, although she wanted to offer to make him a list of girls that she approved of.

It wouldn't be a long one. Sweet Water had more than its share of women of character and integrity, but there weren't a lot of personalities that would fit with Mav's. He needed someone steady and solid. Someone who would anchor him and who wouldn't be afraid to challenge him if he needed it. He had a tendency to be a little lazy and not live up to his potential, preferring the easy route over hard work.

The door closed behind him, and as though Howard could read her thoughts, he squeezed her shoulders, turning her around so he could tuck her against his chest and under his chin. Wrapping his arms around her as she leaned into his warmth and strength.

"God knows. He's got the best girl picked out for him. We just have to trust."

"I trust God. But I'm afraid that Mav is going to run ahead of Him, like he has so many times before."

"If he's truly turning over a new leaf, he won't. And you know that. I'm praying, and I'm sure you are too."

"I am. And you're right. Whatever happens, even if it seems like it's a catastrophe, God can use it. I just have to pull my hands away and allow things to work out."

"Easier said than done."

She wrapped her arms around his waist and held him close. Wasn't that the truth.

Chapter 6

Cassie walked home, every step feeling like her shoes were filled with lead.

She wanted to go, find Mav, tell him she would marry him, tell him that's what she'd always wanted, and beg him to pick her.

But that wasn't keeping her word to the Lord. So she directed her steps toward home, reminding herself that she had a big project to do, that she was blessed to have work, that she was blessed to have life and breath, and to enjoy what God had given her, without thinking that she deserved more somehow.

She'd barely gone into her house and gotten a cup of coffee made and poured, carrying it into her office, before there was a quick rap on her door, and then it burst open.

She stuck her head out of her office door, looking down the hall toward the front door where Teagan stood in her house, looking breathless and disheveled and calling out, "Cassie! Cassie! You won't believe what I just heard!"

It was amazing that they hadn't passed each other in town, as small as Sweet Water was and as closely as Teagan had followed her into the house.

"I'm here," Cassie said, stepping out of her office and walking down the hall.

"Oh my goodness, Cassie. You won't believe it."

Teagan was one of the few people who knew about Cassie's crush. Knew that she had a thing for Mav for years. She also knew that Mav had never had the time of day for her.

"Mav is trying to find a wife!"

"Trying?" She would have thought he'd have found one by now. She had figured Teagan had come to tell her about his wedding, except Teagan looked excited, and she probably wouldn't look so happy if she had bad news.

"Yes. Still trying." She grinned. "It's Mav, so of course he announced it, then promptly left town, and no one has been able to find him. Finally, someone got a hold of him, found out he was at his mom's, and he's on his way back to the diner where he's going to hold court."

"Hold court?"

"To interview all the women who want to marry him!" Teagan said. There didn't seem to be any sarcasm in her voice, as if she, like Cassie, believed that there would be so many women Mav would have a hard time choosing.

"I heard something similar. That he was trying to find a girl to marry today." Cassie couldn't keep the depression out of her voice. And Teagan's face fell.

"Then why aren't you there? With bells on? Do you want me to help you fix your hair? We can do your makeup. I'll help you pick out something to wear?" Teagan grabbed her hand, her smile back on her face, but it slowly faded as she studied Cassie. "You're not going to try, are you?"

"I can't. You know what I promised."

"God put this opportunity right in front of you!"

"No. It's a temptation. I can't go and fix my hair, put on special clothes, and run out, clawing and scratching and trying to get to the front of the line just so Mav will pick me. That's not what I said I would do."

From the look on Teagan's face, it was clear she hurt for Cassie. Teagan wanted the very best for her, wanted her to have her heart's desire, and would fight as hard as she could for her. It made Cassie smile.

She lifted up the hand that Teagan held and clasped her other hand around it. "God has shown me over the last year what people really are my friends. The ones who help me be better. I was chasing after a dream. Giving all of my energy to someone who didn't even care for me, when there were all these people who loved me and cared for me right here. I just didn't want to see them. I wanted something that God didn't want for me. And I said I wasn't going to chase after it anymore. And, well, I shouldn't. Because if I had been, maybe you and I wouldn't have grown closer over this last year."

"I admire your walk with God," Teagan said, but it almost sounded like she was holding her impatience in check. "But can't you let loose just a little bit? I mean, can't you see that this might be something that God really wants you to do?"

"I can pray about it. But I already feel like I shouldn't. It's not that I don't want to compete with all the other girls. It's that I know it isn't the right way."

"How could it not be the right way? How can you know that?"

"Don't you just have the feeling sometimes that something isn't right? Don't you just know that it's just not lining up with what you said you would do or what you promised? Even if I didn't exactly promise that if Mav ever offered to sit at the diner and go through a line of women who were willing to marry him, that I wouldn't go, that's not the point. It's the idea that God knows what I meant, and this is not it."

Teagan pressed her lips together and looked away. Cassie wasn't sure whether it was to marshal her arguments or to give up the hope that she had and admit Cassie was right.

Either way, she knew Teagan would stand by her, even if she didn't do what Teagan thought she should.

After all, Teagan might say that she needed to put her dedication to the Lord aside, but she didn't really mean it. She wanted Cassie to follow God.

And after the cancer, after facing the idea of her own mortality, after knowing that she could die, she knew how badly she needed God. More than she needed Mav. More than she wanted Mav, although at times, it didn't seem possible.

"No. I said that I wouldn't chase after him. Getting all dolled up and going to the diner to stand in line is chasing. If God provides a way that isn't pushing and scrambling, then, okay. I'm in. Last year this time, I would have jumped on this opportunity, but I can't go back on my promise."

"I hope that God knows what He has in you. I just hope He blesses you to the point where you totally get everything you deserve."

"Then I wouldn't have anything. Because I deserve nothing."

"That's not true! Even before you made this vow, you put God first in every decision you made. Even though it means potentially not getting what you've wanted since you were, what? Fifteen?"

"I think I might have been even younger," Cassie said, squinching up her face, a little embarrassed. She had crushed on Mav ever since she could remember. There had never been anyone else that she had been the slightest bit interested in. It had only ever been him.

"All right. I can see your mind is set. Mav is saying that he's already talked to the preacher and the preacher is going to be at the church at eleven thirty tonight. For some reason, it's extremely important that he be married by midnight. So, he's invited the whole town to his wedding."

"So, he did pick someone?" Cassie said, a little confused, because she thought Teagan had been talking like Mav hadn't made a decision yet.

"No. He hasn't. But he said he's going to, even though I didn't see anyone waiting in line when I went by the diner." Teagan shrugged, like that was a minor detail.

"So today is Mav's wedding day," Cassie said, feeling a heavy weight in her chest, like she wanted to go lie down, just sleep until the nightmare was over.

"Are you going to come to the wedding?"

Cassie started to shake her head, but then she thought that maybe it would be more real and she would heal faster if she actually saw the nuptials. It would be like daggers in her heart, but again, not as bad as it would have been last year this time when she had put all of her stock into her infatuation with Mav.

"I think I might," she said and tried to smile.

"Then let's do a makeover. Let's get you fixed up. I'll call Abrielle and Zaylee, who's exactly your size, and between us, we can get you clothes, fix your hair, do your makeup, and make you look beautiful." Teagan grinned. "Not like you can improve upon perfection, because you look gorgeous now, but you'll feel more confident with the right clothes and the right 'do."

Cassie couldn't argue with that, and she was so grateful to her friend. If it weren't for Teagan, she probably wouldn't even have tried to work but would have gone to bed, hiding under the covers.

This was so much better, to spend the day in celebration, rather than in mourning.

The chains really would be broken, since once Mav was pledged to someone else, she would not be interested in him. And she would be free to serve God with her whole heart. If He never had a man for her, that would have to be perfectly fine. She would just do whatever God wanted her to.

Chapter 7

M av looked at his watch, trying not to panic.

It was five o'clock, and the smells from the kitchen of the diner were simply amazing. Unfortunately, they didn't make up for the fact that there hadn't been a single woman who had taken him up on his offer all day.

He'd gotten up, because he couldn't stand to just sit around, and walked the streets a few times. Up and down, as though him being out and about and available for women to look at would somehow make them decide they wanted to marry him.

He realized, in hindsight, which was always better for him than thinking before he did anything, that this was a colossally stupid idea.

But he was still just stubborn enough to not mention the money. He couldn't. Wouldn't. If they didn't want him for who he was, he wasn't going to mention the money, and he would simply put the ranch on the market tomorrow and go find a job. He wouldn't even try to save it. He'd get the cattle sold and get out of the ranch what he had in it. He wouldn't even try to make a profit. Maybe he'd even leave Sweet Water. It wasn't like he wanted to stick around in a town where no one wanted him.

He knew that was unreasonable.

Just because a woman didn't want to walk up to him and marry him the same day didn't mean that no one wanted him.

His mom and stepdad had been by again. And Jane, the owner of the diner, had come over to his table several times. Giving him coffee, offering him a taste of the new dessert she had tried, and asking if he would taste a new type of chicken she was making.

He'd agreed, because his stomach was growling. Even when he was in the depths of despair, he could eat.

He'd never had anything hit him so hard that he lost his appetite.

"You'll have to tell me if this is any good," Jane said as she set a plate of what looked like smothered chicken in front of him.

"All right. Although, I'm not real picky, so there isn't much I don't like. No offense or anything." He realized that maybe he shouldn't have said it quite like that. He also realized that Jane was single and had watched him sit there all day.

"No one's come by?"

"Not yet. I haven't lost hope, though." He grinned, engagingly, even if he couldn't find any words to flirt with.

He didn't really want to be a flirt anymore. If he was someone who was considering marriage, flirting shouldn't be something he was practicing. But maybe marriage wasn't going to work out after all.

"Well, I hope someone does, for your sake," Jane said, giving him a little smile.

"What about you?" he asked before he could stop the words from tumbling out.

"Oh my goodness. You don't want me. I have two little girls, first of all. I'm also most likely older than you are. By a good five years or so."

"It wouldn't matter," he said, but she was right. The children he wouldn't mind, but Jane was busy running the restaurant. She hadn't stopped all day since he'd come in. Cooking, cleaning, waiting tables, making it all work. She did have help, but the woman hadn't taken a breather all day. She would make an excellent rancher's wife, but she would have to give up the diner. He highly doubted she would do that. But it had been worth a shot.

"I think you'd get tired of me. Plus, I'm living and breathing the diner right now, and that's not what you need." She gave him another small smile, and he knew she was right.

If he stopped to examine his feelings, he was actually relieved she hadn't taken him up on it. It would suit his pride, sure, but the words of his mother, that it would be better to be single than to be stuck with the wrong girl, echoed in his head, and he didn't say anything else. Other than, "If this tastes as good as it smells, it's going to be delicious."

"I hope. I keep tinkering with things, because it just lacked a little bit of something. I couldn't quite put my finger on it. But I think that's what I'm going to be teaching the men on Sunday. If... If you want to come, you're welcome."

He appreciated her kindness. She'd been sweet to him all day, and even though she didn't want to marry him, she hadn't laughed at him or made fun of him for sitting here, expecting some woman to come up to him and announce that she would take him.

The least he could do was come to her cooking class.

"I'll be there," he said. It might be the last day he spent in Sweet Water, but he'd stay until Sunday at least so that he could keep his word and go to Jane's cooking class.

He dug into the chicken, which tasted good to him, although he agreed with her, there was something missing in the ingredients. He wasn't sure exactly what. But he'd think about it and maybe be able to come on Sunday with a good recommendation.

Not that he cooked that much, but he'd been on the harvest crew, and some years they hadn't had a cook, so the guys had taken turns. Some years, he smiled fondly, they had a terrible cook. Reina, Preacher's wife, had cooked for the one year, and they probably would have been better off cooking for themselves, since she had no clue what she was doing.

Still, she was sweet and tried her best, and that's all Preacher had needed. He'd fallen head over heels with her and married her before the year was out.

Mav always thought that maybe something like that would happen to him, but it hadn't.

The hours ticked by, slowly, and Mav was tempted to get up and go home. But he said he would be at the diner until eleven thirty when he walked to the church to have his wedding.

He intended to fulfill his promise, and if there ended up being no bride, then he'd done his very best. He couldn't think of anything else to do, other than to start knocking on doors, and that seemed a little...desperate.

Jane usually closed the diner at eleven, but she left it open for an extra half an hour so he could stay at his table. He appreciated it, but while there was a crowd, there was still no bride.

Finally, at eleven twenty-five, he pushed back away from the table, looking around at all the people who stared at him.

A couple of his brothers were there. They were smirking more than the other men, but he considered them his best friends, and he knew they were pulling for him. Even if they did think he was immature.

This was probably just another case in point.

He'd started the day promising God that he was going to be better, and then look at him. He'd wasted the day waiting for something that was never meant to happen.

"Where's your bride, Mav?" a man from the back of the crowd in the diner called out.

"I guess I feel like you must have been paying women to stay away from me today."

The crowd laughed, and Mav had his devil-may-care grin firmly in place, but embarrassment clawed at the back of his throat, and it took courage to stand, face the crowd and his failure, and walk toward the door as the crowd parted for him.

"Maybe you should have offered to pay someone. You might have had more luck," someone else called.

If they only knew. He could have paid them. One billion dollars. But he chose not to. Throughout the day, he'd been so tempted to go back on that, but each time he had considered it, something had told him no.

Just trust.

And while he didn't exactly know what he was waiting and trusting for, he knew that blabbing about the money wasn't the way he wanted to go. Not this time.

"Well, it's time for me to be at the church." He wanted to skip it. Wanted to just go home and crawl in bed and admit defeat. It was the biggest defeat of his life and the biggest mistake too.

Why had he put that letter aside? He would have worked a lot harder at finding a woman if he would have known that there was one billion dollars in it for him.

Them.

He had to start remembering that he wasn't the only person in the world.

He'd never get married if he just continuously put himself first. Deciding he was going to go through with it, feeling like there was a reason he needed to walk to the church, he pushed the door open, waved a hand at Jane, who was picking up his cup from the counter, and walked out into the night.

North Dakota nights were notoriously cold, and this one was no different. After the sun went down, and especially when the night sky was clear, the chill descended, but he loved that chill. Loved the way it made the whole world feel fresh and clear and clean.

It didn't take away his problems, but it did bolster him some as he walked silently to the church, hearing the murmur of the crowd behind him, some of the people laughing and saying they knew he wasn't going to actually get anyone. That they had told their sister or daughter or friend that he was not a good bet.

And they were most likely right.

If he was going to learn anything out of this, one lesson would be that a good reputation took more than a couple of hours to build. He had been a flake all of his life. He couldn't just have a moment with God and think that everyone was going to see that he was changed.

Especially when he didn't. He had acted the way he had always acted, rushing in headlong and doing something crazy.

But it felt like the right thing to do. Sometimes that crazy thing *was* the right thing.

He got to the church, surprised to see there were cars in the lot. In fact, it was almost full.

Opening the back door and walking in through the vestibule, he saw that the church was actually packed. It was almost like a Christmas Eve service.

Great. Now the entire town could see his humiliation.

Still, he couldn't bring himself to turn around and walk out, even if he could with the people who were streaming in behind him.

The folks who had stayed at the diner to watch the show there were the folks who were going to struggle to get a seat, and he almost laughed at that.

The pastor stood at the front of the church, his Bible and Holy ceremony book open in front of him. He was ready at least. He had said he would do it, and he had kept his word. Not that Mav had expected anything less from him. Of course the pastor would do what he said he was going to do.

Unsure what he was going to do when he got to the front where the preacher waited, he started up the aisle, looking from side to side.

To his surprise, he saw his mother there.

She, understandably, looked a little worried. But she gave him a tumultuous smile.

He saw Preacher sitting with his arm around Reina, their children filling out the row. Older now, teenagers.

Preacher was almost done with his child-raising years, and Mav hadn't even started. Of course, Preacher was ten years older than him too.

Still, he'd spent a lot of time messing around, focusing on things that really didn't matter. He could see that now. When he got home, he was going to have a long discussion with God, then he was going to get his Bible out and figure out where he was going to start reading. Because it was going to be a regular thing from now on. He'd promised, and he wasn't the kind of person who went back on a promise.

Dread pooled in his stomach, and he felt a little like he was going to throw up. The chicken had been good, but he wished he hadn't eaten it. Even if it had been almost six hours ago. Jane had brought him seconds, and when he tried to pay, she waved him away, saying that he brought more business to the diner than she'd had in a long time, and she appreciated it.

Maybe she came in the back after him to watch with everyone else. Maybe she didn't. He supposed it didn't matter. She was smarter than he was, to know that they weren't a good fit.

With that thought in mind, he really didn't know who *would* have been a good fit. He certainly didn't have anyone in mind. He'd never met anyone he liked well enough to get him to the point where he felt like he couldn't live without them.

That's what he'd always imagined love to be. Some kind of deep feeling where he was overwhelmed with emotion and crazed with the idea of being without the object of his affection. And she would feel the same. Almost hero worship. Or something like that.

He wasn't even sure, just knew that his idea of love probably wasn't a biblical one. Not from the teaching that he had on it, but he bought into what the world said, that love was a mushy-gushy feeling, and he should have butterflies and rainbows sparkling around.

He supposed none of the girls that he dated had ever stuck around for the butterflies and rainbows part.

Which was too bad.

A few more steps and he was at the front. The lights were dim, kind of like they were for a Christmas Eve service, and candles had been lit. Probably some woman with romantic thoughts in mind thinking she would create the perfect atmosphere for a wedding.

Except, there wasn't going to be a wedding, because there was no bride.

He'd never miscalculated this badly in his life before, and he wished with all his heart that he could go to bed, wake up, and have a do-over. He would certainly do today a lot different, of course. If he could have a do-over, he might as well start when he was about fifteen. He could have a do-over at that point and live his life a lot differently than he had.

He stopped in front of the preacher. The preacher had a bit of a confused look on his face.

"Where's your bride?" the preacher asked, smiling a little, like he was used to brides being late.

"I guess she'll be turning up here shortly," Mav said, and the hush of the sanctuary suddenly erupted into excited murmurs.

Everyone must have thought that he had someone waiting. He didn't want them to have misunderstood him like that.

"I actually don't have one," he said in a louder voice. "If I'm going to get married tonight, God's going to have to provide the bride. I've provided the groom."

There, the sanctuary hushed for all of five seconds before it erupted again.

He stood, staring stoically at the front of the pulpit, kicking himself for being the stupidest person in the world.

What was he thinking?

A change in the atmosphere around him, and the murmurs of the crowd, and of electricity in the air made him want to turn around.

He couldn't imagine what people were doing. Maybe getting out in the aisle to make fun of him. Maybe a couple was coming up to renew their vows. He didn't know. But he wasn't going to turn around and see. He would stand here until midnight, and then he would send everyone home. He had done everything he could do to fill the requirements of the letter today.

Of course, it would have been nice if he could have started back when he got the letter, years ago, but no point in wishing.

The pastor shifted in front of him, almost as though he were moving to stand between two people, and his eyes narrowed while his brows drew down.

Mav turned his head slightly as a person stepped into his peripheral vision.

She walked slowly, sedately, her head up, her stride unhurried, like she was confident in herself and in what she was doing.

His gaze hooked on her hair at first, falling in waves around her shoulders, and then the dress that flowed around her legs. Like a whisper on the breeze.

His eyes tracked up, seeing the indent of her waist, her long, slender neck on top of curves that looked just perfect.

Then, his eyes caught on her face.

He didn't recognize her at first, she looked...different than he'd ever seen her. He knew her name. He couldn't remember it right off, but she was Teagan's friend, someone who lived in town.

That girl who had cancer.

She lifted her chin, probably responding to the absolute lack of welcome or recognition in his face, then she looked at the preacher.

"If you're waiting for his bride, she's arrived."

Chapter 8

Cassie clasped her hands in front of her tightly, trying to disguise the fact that they were trembling almost uncontrollably.

She couldn't look at Mav.

The blank look toward her when she had walked up beside him hurt. He didn't even recognize her.

She wanted to cry. But it had taken all the bravery she possessed to walk up; she wasn't going to turn around and walk away.

Plus, as hard as it was, as much as she hadn't wanted to take the risk of standing up and humiliating herself, it felt like the right thing.

Standing in line and hoping to be the one chosen was her chasing after him, but her walking out, stepping out into the aisle, saving him from embarrassment, almost making a sacrifice, felt exactly right. It didn't go against what she had told God she wouldn't do. In fact, it complemented it.

Funny how the difference was small but stark. One had required her waiting, having faith, not moving until the moment was right. The other one would have allowed her to do whatever she wanted to do, which was rush to the diner and beg him to marry her.

She was so very thankful for Teagan and Zaylee and Abrielle who had come and done her hair and makeup. Teagan had been right, she felt so much more confident knowing she looked as good as she possibly could.

She wasn't the kind of girl who ran around unable to go anywhere without her makeup on, but a little bit gave her confidence that she was presenting the very best front she could.

The fact that Mav didn't even know who she was had knocked her back, more than she wanted to admit.

"All right. If we're going to have this done before midnight, we need to get started," the pastor said, looking at first Cassie and then Mav.

Mav nodded, his face completely serious, and looked at Cassie, with one brow lifted.

Almost as though he were asking her if she was sure.

She hadn't gotten out in front of all these people just to change her mind.

"Clasp right hands, please," the pastor intoned.

Cassie didn't want to, because her hand trembled and was ice cold, but she pulled it from her other hand and set it in Mav's outstretched hand.

His was warm, rough with calluses, and much larger than hers, closing around her fingers, making her feel small and dainty, even.

It wasn't an altogether unpleasant feeling, but she didn't want to be reminded of their differences. She wanted there to be something in common between them. Something that made the sharp feeling inside of her settle down, good and solid.

The pastor droned on, but it was the fastest wedding that Cassie had ever attended.

She supposed when she was a little girl, she dreamed of dressing up in a pretty dress and having flowers and looking like a princess.

This was quite a bit removed from any childish dreams, when her groom acted like he didn't even know her.

He wasn't looking at her with a longing to cherish her, to love her, and to keep her for all time, even though he made those promises.

She didn't know what kind of man Mav was; she only knew what she had built him up to be in her head. Knew what she'd seen of him around town. Knew what she'd heard people saying, but whether he was the kind of man who would make surface promises, just to get married like he said he would? She didn't know.

By the time the pastor pronounced them man and wife, she was struggling so much she was afraid she would not be able to continue to stand.

She couldn't wait to get home and sit down. To get away from all the prying eyes and think about what she had done.

Lord. This seemed like the right thing at the time. Did I just make a huge mistake?

Talk about cold feet.

Mav turned her toward him as the pastor said he could kiss his bride.

She couldn't believe he was going to kiss her and didn't even know her name.

Well, he probably knew it now if he'd been paying attention to the pastor. The pastor knew her name.

His mouth descended, and in shock, she watched it. He was. He was going to kiss her. He hadn't known her name five minutes ago, and now he was going to kiss her.

The idea made her angry. She wasn't even sure why. Maybe it was the idea that Mav would kiss anybody with willing lips standing near him.

That wasn't the kind of man she wanted. She wanted a man who only wanted her. Just her. Not the kind of man who thought any woman would do. But a man who was judicious and fell in love just once. Who didn't kiss, or even flirt with, women.

She was so upset, she turned her head at the last moment, and he ended up bussing her cheek.

He lifted his head as the crowd cheered, or maybe jeered, or maybe it was a combination of both. Regardless, his eyes seemed to search hers, as though wondering why she would have turned her head.

Could he really not know? Did he really think she would welcome the kiss of a man who barely knew her?

Of course he did. After all, she was the one who had gotten out of her seat and volunteered to marry him in the first place. He had every right to expect that she would want to kiss him and...do other things.

The idea made her throat close with panic.

Surely not. Surely he wasn't expecting that. Not tonight. Goodness. She wasn't expecting to be married ten minutes ago, and now she was hitched to the man of her dreams, but in her dreams, he cherished her. He loved her and respected her and wanted every good thing for her.

In reality, she wasn't sure what he wanted.

"Ladies and gentlemen, may I present to you, Mr. and Mrs. Mav Stryker." The pastor's voice carried throughout the room, and cheers went up.

"You said you were going to do it, and I guess you did," a man's voice lifted up above the crowd.

Mav grinned, but he didn't say anything, holding tightly to her hands.

He leaned down to her ear. "We need to go somewhere and talk."

No kidding.

They should have been talking before this. But she nodded her head in agreement, and he tugged on her hand, leading her down the aisle.

Her skirt swished around her legs, soft and light and making her feel like a princess, even if the evening hadn't quite turned out that way.

She caught Teagan's eye as she walked by. Teagan was giving her a thumbs-up, her other hand hooked securely in Deuce's arm.

They had moved to Fargo, and Cassie said a silent prayer of thanks that Teagan just happened to be home visiting today. She knew she wouldn't have gone to the church if Teagan hadn't shown up and then called reinforcements.

She would thank her, but later. Not now. Not as Mav pulled her out of the church, down the front stairs.

"Where do you live?" he asked as he made his way into the parking lot, toward his pickup.

"Just a few houses down. We could walk."

He stopped, looking down at her.

"I think I know you." He pursed his lips. "You're the girl that had cancer."

She wanted to close her eyes as hurt swam through her. Yes. She was the girl who had cancer.

Yes. He knew her.

Yes. He crushed her spirit just a little bit at a time.

Lord, did You think I needed a growing opportunity? Is this how the next fifty years are going to be? Me closing my eyes against the pain because he doesn't know me, doesn't care for me, doesn't know anything about me, and isn't interested in learning?

She shouldn't complain. God had given her the desire of her heart. She remembered all the warnings though, warnings that sometimes God allowed people to have what they wanted, just to teach them a lesson.

This was going to be a hard, long lesson.

Of course, they weren't really married.

"You'll have to show me. Because I don't know."

Mav's words were terse, like he was eager to get away, and she couldn't blame him. He'd been in the spotlight all day. Of course, it had been a spotlight of his own making. He was the one who had announced that he was getting married by the end of the day. And now, since he hadn't refused her when she had stepped forward, she knew that he actually didn't have a bride.

It was an odd game to play.

One she probably should not have participated in.

People spilled out of the church behind them. She could hear them laughing on the sidewalk as they walked further away, Mav still holding her hand, but it didn't feel good. Didn't feel like he was holding it because he loved her and wanted to. Didn't feel like their skin rubbed together and her skin touched the skin of someone she loved and who she knew was going to use those hands to work to protect her and to take care of her and to cherish her.

It wasn't like that at all. It felt more like he had to, so he was.

She tried to shake that feeling. She couldn't go into her marriage judging him and finding him lacking. She had to find things that were positive and focus on them.

Determined to make the best of this, she squared her shoulders and tried to think the best about the evening and about Mav.

Mav was brave. He was bold. She'd already known that and loved that about him.

He wasn't afraid to take risks, and he hadn't let go of her hand. That had to mean something. Maybe that meant that now that they were joined together, he wasn't going to let her go. Was going to make sure that she was cared for at the very least.

She chose to believe that.

"This is my house," she said, pointing to her porch and the steps, hearing Phyllis barking on the other side of the door.

"Sounds like you have a man-eater in there."

"She's quite ferocious. All fifteen pounds of her," Cassie said, trying to dredge up a real smile, glad that her legs weren't shaking quite as much as they had been when they'd been standing in front of everyone.

She didn't keep her door locked, and it was a simple matter of opening it, pushing a screen door, and making sure Phyllis didn't run out behind her. Pulling her hand from Mav's, she scooped Phyllis up while he closed the door behind them.

"I hope it's okay to say this, but I'm glad to be behind closed doors. I felt like I was in a fishbowl all day. There have been a lot of times in my life where I've had a lot of eyes on me, but today was the worst."

"I bet it was. You... You really didn't know who you were going to marry when you announced that you were going to get married?"

"No. I didn't." He stared at her, his eyes a little hooded, some mystery in there that she wanted to tease out.

"Can I get you something to drink?"

"Sure. Coffee would be great."

"At this time of night?"

"Yeah. I'm not going to sleep anyway, and I can use the caffeine. It might make the headache go away."

"I could get you some pain medicine?"

He kept his mouth closed for a minute, then said, "All right. Water and pain medicine."

She smiled, not knowing what to think but inwardly pleased that he had changed his mind at her suggestion.

Maybe he wasn't going to be completely impossible to work with after all.

Not that she necessarily thought he was, she just wasn't sure how he was going to treat her.

Keep a positive outlook. Believe the best. Look at him and see the very best. Don't see the things that hurt you, see the things he's doing right.

That voice was right. And she knew it. So, she got the pain meds out and filled the glass with ice and water, and set them both in front of him at the table before she took her seat. All the time, she reminded herself to look at the good.

"Thank you," he said as he picked up the pills and then the glass.

There seemed to be lines of strain around his eyes and a tightness around his mouth as she watched him, and she wondered if it was just from being in the fishbowl, as he had called it, today, or if there was something else.

Despite herself, her heart felt soft and tender toward him, and she wanted to help. To ease his burden. To make his life easier.

She couldn't believe herself, even after the man didn't recognize her but married her anyway, that she would have those feelings toward him.

Then she reminded herself, positive thoughts. And she remembered how he had carried her along with him as he had walked away. Had known immediately that they needed to communicate, wanting to talk to her, hopefully about what they were going to do since they didn't really have a legal marriage.

"Thanks," he said again after he had drained the glass and set it back down on the table. "I don't know why I'm so thirsty and my head is pounding. I guess it's been a day."

"They should start to work in fifteen or twenty minutes," she said softly, knowing how often she herself had taken pain medicine and then stared at the clock, waiting and watching, counting the seconds until it started to take effect.

"Why did you step out?" he asked. That wasn't how she was expecting to have the conversation start out.

If he thought she was going to be vulnerable when he hadn't been, he had a new thought coming.

But then she remembered, she couldn't expect tit for tat. She had to be willing to give more.

She took a breath. Maybe she felt like she had already given more. Since she was the one who had taken the risk, and he was the one who didn't know her, but it didn't matter. Marriage wasn't I gave so now it's your turn. She didn't want to start out that way.

"There were probably a lot of reasons why I stepped out. One of them was because I realize you didn't have someone already planned. And you were waiting for someone to do exactly what I did. So I figured, why not me?"

There. She answered his question, even if she didn't tell the entire truth. She gave accurate but not complete information.

Before he could ask her for anything more, she said, "You know the marriage isn't legal? We didn't have a license."

Chapter 9

Mav's eyes widened as they met Cassie's, realization entering them.

"You're right. I never even thought about a license. The pastor mentioned it, and I assured him I'd get one. That was this morning, and I completely forgot."

"I can't believe the pastor agreed to marry us without one. But I've heard of other people doing that. Where they forgot to get the license, or they were unable to. The pastor marries them, then they get the license at the courthouse later." She lifted her shoulder. "In the eyes of God, we're married, of course. We said vows. They're just as binding without a license as with. But to make it legal, we need a license."

"We can do that first thing tomorrow," he said immediately, then he froze, his eyes flying to hers, as though he just remembered that she was there, and he said, "That's okay with you?"

She smiled, appreciating the fact that he was at least trying to include her. His reputation was that he was out for himself, not in a bad way, necessarily, just an immature, I haven't grown up enough to think about others kind of way.

"Yes. If we're actually going to do this, I think that's a smart thing to do." She wasn't sure what the law was, wasn't sure if it was the pastor's duty or theirs to get everything filed legally, but they could figure it out.

"Did you consider it not legit?" he asked, his tone dripping with surprise.

"No. I don't make vows lightly, but...I wasn't sure about you." That wasn't entirely fair. She was sure about him, mostly.

One side of his mouth pulled back, and his head tilted to one side. "That's fair. That's my reputation."

He put one hand around his glass and watched his thumb slice through the condensation on it.

"I have every intention of keeping them. But it's only fair that you know that I don't have a very good track record when it comes to relationships... I'm not sure exactly what I do wrong, but I—" He broke off, then looked her square in the eye. "This morning... I guess you could call it a rededication. I rededicated myself to God. I hadn't been putting Him first in my life, not like I should. I've been living for myself." He laughed. "I suppose it's kind of crazy that I did that, and then later today, I did something crazy like announce to the town that I was going to get married, without knowing who my wife was going to be. But...I guess I should tell you why."

"There's a reason? It wasn't something that's just typical Mav Stryker?"

"You talk like you know me. But I'm pretty sure we've never spoken."

"You were older than me in school. And yes. I know you. Everybody in Sweet Water does," she said that last part in her defense so he wouldn't think she followed his every move like some lovesick puppy. Which was basically what she had done—followed his every move like a lovesick puppy.

He nodded, accepting that answer. "You have an advantage over me, because I really don't know you, other than you did have cancer, right?"

"Yeah. I'm that girl who had cancer."

"Are you still taking treatments?" he asked, his face scrunched up, his eyes holding concern, which surprised her. She would have thought he would be annoyed if she were still going through treatment. It might mess up his plans.

"No. I was declared cured. Although I have more chance than a normal person of having it return at some point in my life."

"All right. I guess we'll cross that bridge, and fight that battle, when we get there."

That warmed her heart. He probably didn't even realize how much the idea of him helping her fight her battle made her feel. It wasn't just one person, it was two. And two people together were much stronger than one person alone. She felt it, and she knew it to be true.

That statement alone was enough to melt all of her defenses, but she didn't let her guard down. There had to be more. And she could imagine that there was going to be more pain involved, because her emotions were involved, while he didn't care about her one way or the other. Other than she was his wife. And he apparently was going to honor that commitment. However that looked to him.

"That's fair," she finally said when he seemed to be waiting for her to say something.

"All right. I got a letter. A couple of years ago actually, and I threw it in a drawer." He looked sheepish. "But after I rededicated my life to the Lord this morning, I just felt an urge to look in the drawer, and I lifted a bunch of other junk that I had stuffed in there, and this letter was on top. Just lying there."

"All right," she prompted when he didn't say anything more for a bit.

"I got it out and opened it, and...maybe I should just let you read it. I took a picture of it on my phone. You might have a little bit of trouble seeing it, but why don't we just do that."

He handed her his phone. It was dark. He hadn't pulled it up or anything.

She tilted it so that the screen lit up, and then he told her his password.

That surprised her. But she liked it. That there wouldn't be secrets between them. That she would know the password to his phone and be able to access what was on it at any time. He had surprised her again, in the very best way, and she said a silent prayer of thanks that God had orchestrated that to warm and touch her heart. He wouldn't hide things from her, he was going to be transparent.

Especially since he could hardly have gone through his phone and deleted everything, thinking that he would eventually be handing it to her this evening. Although, if he was confident that he would get married, maybe he had.

She tried not to make it mean more than what it did, but she couldn't deny it meant a lot to her.

He directed her to his camera app, and she pulled up the last picture, which was the letter. She read it in silence. Then, unbelieving, she read it again.

Slowly her hand holding the phone fell to the table, and she looked up into his eyes. "Is this a joke?"

It said one billion. It had to be a joke.

"I had my stepdad check out the lawyer's office. He said it was legit. I couldn't get a hold of the lawyer's office when I tried to call... It did say it was a...petting zoo."

"A what?" She thought he said petting zoo. She was tempted to laugh, but he looked extremely uncomfortable.

"Uh, a petting zoo. It said I had reached a petting zoo *and* the law office, so I left a message. Honestly, my stepdad is really astute in these kinds of things, and he did say it was legit. I promise."

"I believe you. And remember, I didn't know about the money when I married you. This is a surprise, and it would be a really nice thing to have happen, but it doesn't make any difference to me." She looked at him, her chin down, her eyes drilling into his.

He nodded.

"I know." He smiled a little. "The old me would have told the town about the money immediately. Maybe not. I wanted someone to step out in faith and marry me, and not because of the money. You didn't need the money to take a chance on me. Don't you think that I'll ever forget that."

There were a lot of faults that were associated with Mav Stryker, but a lack of loyalty was never one of them. She believed that he would be loyal to her until he died.

She liked that. She was loyal herself and valued it in others. Loved that the man she had married had that as one of his dominant characteristics.

She returned his smile, and they just looked into each other's eyes for a moment. She would love to know what he was thinking. Was he trying to manipulate her? Was he trying to gauge his next words so that she would react the way he wanted her to? Or was he liking what he saw? Did he admire her and think that he had made a good decision? Was he glad she had stepped out?

She wanted all of those questions and more answered but knew they were not going to be answered tonight, or maybe never. Not anytime soon anyway.

"So, I'll try again tomorrow, and we'll see what we need to do to get the money. Hopefully it doesn't make a difference that we had to get our license on the day after we got married. Because I don't know if you noticed, but the letter expired at midnight yesterday."

It was twelve thirty AM, and yesterday was a half an hour ago.

"That would stink," she said and laughed a little.

He laughed along with her. "You don't say."

They grinned at each other; the laughter had been good for them.

"All right. So now you know why I did something a little crazy. I... I felt like it was a good thing to do. And I see you understand why I didn't mention the money."

"I do. But that's all in the past, I guess I'm wondering where we're going to go from here?"

She didn't mean to drive the conversation or rush him in any way. But it was twelve thirty, and she was tired. It had been a big day, and she couldn't quite believe that she had done what she did.

"Tomorrow I'm going to try to get a hold of the lawyer. It might mean we have to drive there to sign some papers. That would be after we get a license. And I'm not sure what we do about that, but the preacher would know."

"Yeah. He's done it often enough that we can at least ask him. It might be up to him to make things work with the state."

"Yeah. And if we need to have another small ceremony, we can do that. Right?"

"Yes." She tried to think. "I have a project that's due by the end of the week."

"You work."

She managed to not roll her eyes. "Yes. I work."

"What do you do?" he asked. "And where?"

It seemed like he was running through his brain all the places she might be able to work around Sweet Water. The training center had just opened a little northeast of town, and there were people in town who worked there. Maybe he thought that's what she was doing, but she didn't ask.

"A graphic designer. It's what I went to college for. It's what my degree is in. I'm self-employed, so I do projects as I get them, and sometimes it's feast or famine. I'll have a bunch of projects all at once, and then I'll go for a week or two with nothing. So I have to pace myself. Pace my spending."

He was her husband, he deserved that explanation, maybe even more.

"Because of my past history, I don't want to let my health insurance run out. So that's the first thing I pay, even before groceries."

"Well, if this billion-dollar thing is accurate, then you shouldn't have to worry too much about what you pay first every month. We could pay the insurance in a lump sum for the year if we want to."

She smiled. How nice. To have the burden of providing for herself lifted off her shoulders. "I would still want to work. It is satisfying and makes me feel good about myself."

"I... I was hoping you would move out to the ranch."

His words didn't seem as confident as maybe he wanted them to. She looked down. She loved her house. The porch and the little garden she had started outside. The plants and Phyllis. Phyllis was a town dog. She wasn't cut out to be on the farm.

But she thought about Sarah following Abraham, and Rebecca traveling to where Isaac was.

Bathsheba was moved into the palace. And she couldn't think of a single time in the Bible where anyone got married and the husband moved to be with the wife.

She supposed if he wanted to, she would welcome it, but if the choice had to be made, she would have to choose to move.

Or she could be stubborn, but that wouldn't benefit anyone.

"If you're really attached to your house... Maybe we can work something out?"

"I've never lived outside of town before. I'm used to being able to walk wherever I want to. I own a car but don't drive very well, especially in the North Dakota winters."

"I can drive you wherever you need to go. Most of the time, whenever you want. Although, if I'm working cattle that day, it might have to wait until the next day, but you would...be a priority to me."

She hoped that would last for more than just a few months, longer than it took the newlywed bliss to wear off, or whatever it was called.

"All right. I... I'll move. I'll need to get this project done first. I don't want to stop it in the middle. But I can keep from bidding on anything else, although if something that I've already bid on comes up, I'll need to do that. But then I'll start getting ready to move."

It was simple. She could do it. When she stepped out into that aisle, she knew there were going to be things that she was going to have to change if she went through with it, things that she was going to have to do that she might not be ready for. Or things that she'd been ready for all her life.

She was married to Mav Stryker, the man of her dreams. She could do a few little things to make sure that their marriage started out well.

"I don't have too much work to do on the farm right now, I actually was... I was in a pretty tight spot financially, and that's what made me kneel down and tell God that I would do whatever He wanted me to do, if only He would get me out of it." He grinned a little, but his face held all the seriousness that it had that evening. "I meant what I said. I've made promises before to God, and it's kind of easy to be slack concerning those promises. But this time, I'm not going to relax. I am going to do whatever God wants me to do, because He didn't give up on me."

She loved that. That he gave God the credit for the money and the letter and everything that happened, and he believed God loved him and wasn't going to just toss him aside because he hadn't been perfect in the past.

"Wow. That's...inspiring." She wasn't saying it just to make him feel good, she was saying it because it was true.

Chapter 10

M av stretched, exaggerating just a bit. He didn't know how else to broach the subject.

"I guess it's time for us to go to bed." He grinned a little to himself. He always looked forward to having a wife.

It took him about five seconds to realize that her eyes had gotten big, and her hand flew to her chest before she stuttered out, "Us?"

"We're married, aren't we?"

If possible, her eyes got bigger, and she drew back a bit.

"Well, yeah, but up until this point in our lives, we hadn't talked to each other at all. We're...not going to bed together."

She hadn't been that forceful about anything else that she'd said to him yet.

He drew back, surprised. He had just assumed that was what married people did. He hadn't thought that just because they hadn't talked to each other that they weren't going to go to bed together.

Interesting. What caused her to think that they wouldn't? He narrowed his eyes, contemplating her expression, which made him feel like she hated him, which was odd, since up to that point, he hadn't felt that way.

After all, out of all the women in the town, she was the only one who was willing to step out in the aisle and make vows to him.

"I don't think you find me repulsive," he finally said, unsure of what else to say. What was there to say?

She relaxed just a bit, although she didn't smile. "I don't."

"Then..." He wasn't quite sure what to ask, and then he remembered. She was the girl who had cancer.

"Does it have something to do with you having cancer and not being able to...you know?"

Any relaxing that might have happened was quickly reversed as she stiffened, and her horrified expression became offended as well.

"No. That has nothing to do with anything."

She definitely sounded offended now, on top of not seeming to like him at all.

His family always said he stuck his foot in his mouth more than anyone they knew. He didn't mean to, just...didn't know.

"All right. I'm sorry. That upset you, and I'm not sure why."

"Because having cancer seems to be the only thing that anyone ever remembers about me. You included." She added that "you included" after a small pause, almost as though she didn't want to accuse him of anything, or insult him, but just couldn't help it.

"I didn't realize that offended you."

That was true. But he did think of her as the girl who had cancer.

"I didn't mean for it to. If you had orange hair, I would think of you as that girl with the orange hair. Or if you walked Great Danes around the town, I would think of you as that girl with the Great Danes. It's not an insult. It's just fact."

His explanation made her relax some, and he could see that his line of reasoning made sense to her, at least. Sometimes when he tried to explain himself, he ended up sounding more dumb than what he did to begin with. But this was important. He wanted his wife—if she stayed his wife, which, if she wasn't willing to share a bed with him, he wasn't sure where that left them—to know and understand and appreciate where he came from.

"All right. You have a point. I'm sorry. It just...seems like my whole life has been defined by cancer, and I beat it. It's over. I don't want to live the rest of my life being reminded constantly that it's a shadow in my background."

"You said you're more likely to have cancer in the future, since you had it in the past?" That was something he hadn't even considered when he realized who she was. Maybe he wouldn't be married very long. Maybe he'd be married to someone who was in the hospital all the time.

Her lips stayed closed. Like she didn't want to answer, but she stared at him, seeming to be poised on the verge of something, and he waited.

Finally she said, "Yes. I do have a higher chance than a normal person does of having cancer again. Mostly because of the treatments they gave me and not necessarily because I had cancer once. Although, it stands to reason that if it got me once, it will hit me again."

There was something vulnerable about her. Something brave and tremulous about her words, and without thinking, he slid his hand across the table and covered hers. "We'll fight it. Together."

That made her smile. She seemed to like the idea that they were a team. That they would work together.

Wasn't that what a marriage was supposed to be? Two people becoming a team, working together, walking together, doing life together. He liked that idea. Liked the idea of being better together. The two of them. Not the whole world, or the whole country, or even the whole town.

Just Cassie and him, standing shoulder to shoulder against the world.

It was a good picture.

But they had to share a bed too.

"All right. I admit I'm dumb sometimes. And I know it. But I'm willing to learn. If you'll be patient enough to teach me."

"That's something that people always said that I've had a lot of—patience."

"Good. Because you'll probably need it with me."

She smiled, and he felt like that was a good way to open the conversation. Now, he took a breath.

"So, will you tell me what was wrong with my question?"

"Which one? The one of us sleeping together?"

He was glad she was able to look at it head-on. He didn't know what he would have done if she would have made him spell everything out.

"Yeah. That one. For starters anyway. I'm sure I'm going to say other dumb things."

"Like the cancer thing?"

"Yeah. Although you admitted that I had a point there."

"But can you see my point? Do you want to be defined by the thing that you don't want to remember?"

"Like being rejected by every single woman in the entire town?"

He hadn't even begun to process that. Most of the time, he could push things aside and look on the bright side, but it could really do something to a man's ego when he realized that there wasn't a single woman in the entire town who was willing to stand up with him.

Well, there was one. She sat across from him, and he was going to do everything in his power to make sure she didn't regret the decision that she made to walk down the aisle and take his hand.

He didn't know what exactly that was going to entail on his part, but maybe that's something else he should ask her. After she answered the bedroom question.

He waited, brows raised.

"I guess maybe women are a little different than men. But I don't want to sleep with someone that I don't have a relationship with. It would feel...cheap."

He jerked a little bit like he'd been slapped.

"Sleeping with me would feel cheap to you?" He wasn't sure how to respond to that.

"No. I just... I'm just not ready. I don't know you. Don't feel comfortable with you, don't feel like you will be...tender, and I don't know that my secrets are safe with you."

"You have secrets?" He wasn't sure exactly what she was saying, but he was getting the idea that it wasn't just him.

"Not exactly. Just... No one else has ever seen me...in my bedroom. It's not something I do with just anyone. I want to feel comfortable first."

"We're married." He thought that was always the big hang-up. That had been the hang-up for him. It wasn't right to do the married thing without being married. Now that they were married, for him there was no restraint. But apparently for her, it was different.

"All right. I get that you and I are different. Is that a woman vs man thing, or is that just a me being weird thing?"

He was pretty sure it wasn't him being weird. He was pretty sure that men in general, at least all the men that he knew that he had ever talked with about it, felt exactly the same as he did. But as for how women felt, he wasn't sure.

"I'm pretty sure it's a mostly woman thing. I think you could find women who don't feel the same or claim they don't. And feel that sex with anyone, even a stranger, is okay, but I don't feel that way. The Bible clearly says that is something to be enjoyed between a man and woman who are married." She paused. "So...I was thinking eventually. But definitely not tonight."

"We agree on that anyway." He couldn't help feeling disappointed. That had been something he had been looking forward to all day.

"So how long do you think it's going to take you to...feel all the things you said you needed to feel?" he asked, but he figured that was the wrong question when he watched her face scrunch up. Not in revulsion, exactly, but it wasn't that happy, open look that she'd worn for most of the evening.

"I guess it depends on you."

"Me?" If it depended on him, then they'd head into the bedroom right now, together.

"Sure."

He shook his head, lifting his hands. "I'm lost. If it depends on me, we'll go to bed together tonight."

She looked to the side, letting out a breath, not exactly in frustration, but almost of humor. Like she was laughing at how differently they thought.

"I don't even know how to explain to you," she finally said.

"All right. That's fair. I can wait if you think you can find words. Because I'd really like to know."

"We need to have a better relationship first. Talking like we are right now really helps. You handed me your phone earlier and gave me your password. That made a huge difference to me. It meant that you didn't have anything on your phone that you were afraid that I was going to see. And that I can get on your phone anytime I want to. That made a big stride right there."

"That's funny. Because I didn't even know."

"I can give you my phone, you can have my password. But maybe it wouldn't mean the same thing to you."

He held his hand out, and she set her phone in it, telling him her password.

He pushed it in, and sure enough, her phone unlocked. It went to a texting screen, and his eyes caught on one of the messages.

You're married to the man of your dreams! Childhood crush comes true! And then there were some celebration emojis.

Mav flicked her phone off fast, because he knew that text wasn't for his eyes and he didn't want her to know that he'd seen it.

He hadn't even seen who it had come from, but...was that true? Was he really the man of her dreams?

Reeling, but not wanting her to know it, he handed her phone back. "Thanks. I have your password now. It's pretty easy to remember, and I won't forget it."

"You're welcome," she murmured.

He tried to figure out where they had been in the conversation. That seemed to have interrupted him, although if sharing passwords on their phones made her feel like they were developing a relationship, he didn't have a problem with it. Because she was right, there wasn't anything on his phone that he was afraid of her seeing.

His texts were mostly about cattle, pictures of cattle, websites about cattle, conversations about cattle, and a few tractors thrown in for good measure. He might even have a horse among the cows, too.

Nothing else.

Chapter 11

"**S**o, back to what we were talking about. What are our roadblocks?"

Cassie blinked and seemed taken aback, but then she said, "For me, I wouldn't sleep with just anyone. As long as that's something you would do and you don't really care who it's with, then I don't feel like I'm special or that you'll cherish me, so I'm not interested."

Mav raised his brows, because he hadn't really thought about it like that. The idea that it had to be her and no one else. He supposed he'd prefer she think like that about him, although he hadn't thought it until she said it.

"All right. I see. That has to do with building a relationship? What does that entail?"

"Well..." She looked a little baffled, like she never had to think about what constituted building a relationship. "I guess yes, it does. And it's...just sharing ideas and interests. Doing things with each other. That's a good thing. You know, the things you do with all of your friends, that make you feel closer to them, that make you feel like you know you can depend on them and—"

"Wait. A wife is different than a friend."

"But a good marriage is based on friendship. And friendship is based on mutual trust and interest and things that you share."

He hadn't really thought about marriage being based on friendship, but he supposed when he looked at his brothers, and he looked at his mom and stepdad, and the other marriages that he would consider to be good, they seemed to enjoy each other's company. They liked each other, although he wasn't sure exactly what that had to do with being in love. But he could see the friendship being a thing.

"Maybe I'm not a very good friend," he finally said. Maybe that was because it was late, since he didn't usually think about the negative aspects of his personality. But he supposed facing the negatives was the only way to turn them into positives. After all, if a person didn't acknowledge that a negative existed, he could hardly turn it into a positive.

"What makes you say that?" Cassie asked, sounding surprised.

"I don't know. I guess because I've never had a relationship last very long." A couple of months was the longest. But he really didn't want to admit that right now.

"Well, I guess that makes me happy in a way. I suppose you can't really have any skeletons in your closet that I'm going to have to meet eventually if you never had a serious relationship."

"I guess that was because of me, but I always thought it was them. I don't even know what I did to mess things up, but no one ever seemed to want to stay with me for very long."

"Maybe that's because you suggested moving to the bedroom before you could even consider each other friends?"

He grunted, admitting that, while not admitting that that was possible, the idea that he wanted to move into a physical relationship much faster than apparently women were ready for was a distinct possibility.

He didn't typically microanalyze his relationships, but maybe his marriage relationship was one that he really needed to pay attention to.

"So what else?" he asked.

"What else what?" she asked, and he felt a little bad because she did look tired.

Still, he wanted to have some things to think about, but he promised himself this would be the last thing, and then he'd let her go to bed.

Alone, apparently.

"What else builds a relationship?"

"I think that's pretty much it. Talking, talking about important things, not just the weather and what you did that day. More about how you felt about it, what you thought about it, how I feel, and what I think. And being interested in the other person. Like really interested. Wanting to know what they want or like or think. Making the things that are important to them important to you. Responding to them quickly. Stopping what you're doing, and responding immediately, so that they know that they're important to you. Not waiting until the end of the day, or the next day, or whenever to send a reply or waiting until you get home to answer their text or call."

She sighed. "Being able to laugh together. And in my opinion, it just takes time. You can't start talking to someone one day and be instant friends the next. Maybe some people work like that, but I don't. And not because I don't want to, just because it just takes me a little while to warm up to people and to open up and that would be another thing, I guess. Sharing things with people that you don't share with anyone else. Those kinds of things."

He listened, because she said that was part of what it took. He tried to catalog the things that she had listed.

"I might not be able to remember all that. It's apparently not as natural to me as it is to you."

"I think everyone has their abilities. Men and women are different. And I suppose women have dibs on the relationship aspect while men have dibs on other things."

"Such as?"

"Well, you're braver and stronger for one."

"Braver?"

"More open to doing new things. That takes a certain kind of bravery. I wasn't necessarily saying that you're going to go out and slay lions or anything."

"That's a relief."

"I knew you were worried about it, that's why I made sure I got that little bit in."

"Yeah. If I have to defend you with nothing but my fingernails and a toothbrush, I might want to do it against something a little less ferocious than a lion."

"I promise. No lions. I don't even want to see them at the zoo."

"Yeah, that's a little sad. But as I understand it, sometimes they have lions there that wouldn't make it in the wild, so there's that."

"Yeah."

And he supposed that's what she meant. Talking about just everyday things. Deeper than the weather or what they had for supper, and that wouldn't be hard. He could do that.

"All right. I actually really enjoyed talking to you, but I think it's late and you want to go to bed. I guess I'll just drive home."

He started to push back from his chair, but as his hand slipped away from hers, her other hand moved over and came down on top of it.

"Mav. Please wait."

He stopped immediately, looking at her. He thought he was doing a favor by suggesting they go to bed, their separate beds.

"If... If you want to go to bed together, we can." She swallowed hard when she said that, and he figured it took a lot of courage on her part.

He stood still, trying to process.

Finally, he figured he'd just be honest. "I'm sorry, but you are really confusing me. I thought you said we didn't know each other well enough for that."

What was it about women where they said one thing one time, and half an hour later they said the exact opposite thing. It was no wonder he couldn't figure them out.

"I'm sorry. I know I'm not making any sense, at least from your perspective."

"You just completely contradicted yourself, so I think I'm justified in being confused." He wanted to understand. He truly did.

"You are. It's... It's all me. But as we were talking, I was sitting here thinking, you are supposed to be the head of household, and I'm supposed to be submissive. I promised to obey. And that wasn't a hardship, and I don't regret it. It's what the Bible commands me to do. It would be kind of silly for me to think that God doesn't know best. But here I was, thinking I knew better than you and almost lecturing you on how men and women couldn't sleep together until they had a relationship going, and that's not really letting you be the head of the home, is it?" She tilted her head and squinted her eyes at him. Almost as though she were actually asking him.

And he thought that she probably was.

He raised his brows, admitting that she had a point. He hadn't even thought about her taking his authority away from him or not obeying. He hadn't considered that. "I... I don't think you were usurping my authority. I didn't take it that way. I didn't even think about it, because I felt like you were teaching me something I didn't know."

Her eyes widened, but she didn't let go of his hand and her intense look didn't diminish. "Well. Regardless of that. The man is supposed to have the final say. So, if that's what you want, that's what we'll do. And I guess I've lived alone long enough and made my own decisions long enough that I might try to do that again in the future. You know, think I know better than you do, and—"

"There might be times you do know better."

"That's true. I'm not going to argue with that. And I'm not saying anything bad about you. But just sometimes if you have two people, one of them is not going to be right one hundred percent of the time. The thing is, the Bible gives us a hierarchy that we're supposed to adhere to in our marriage, and that doesn't include me telling you that I'm not going to do something, although I guess I could suggest that we not."

"Is that better? A suggestion?" He grinned, liking that she corrected herself without him even realizing that she had stepped aside. Although she was right about God saying that men were the head of the home. That leveled on him a heavy responsibility, answering to an almighty God about how he treated His daughter. Her only responsibility was to obey him.

"Still, that doesn't mean that you can't disagree with me or ask not to do something that I suggest. You had a good point, and while I didn't necessarily feel the same, more for lack of thinking it through than because I don't care, if you can believe that—" She smiled and nodded, and he felt like maybe she actually understood him. Or at least didn't hold him guilty for his lack.

"I think it would be wrong of me to disregard your feelings on the matter. So, in this regard at least, we're going to let things rest on your shoulders, and you can let me know when you're ready, when our relationship has progressed to the point that you feel comfortable sharing a bedroom with me. And that is my authoritative decision on the matter." He said the last part, just in case she was going to argue with him and say that she didn't want to be the one making decisions.

That was the feeling he was getting from looking at her face, and he didn't want that. Didn't want her to think that he wasn't going to take her feelings into consideration.

Wasn't that one of the things that he talked to the Lord about this morning? Not being selfish?

So, while her offer was extremely tempting on one level, on the level where he knew he needed to be living, he didn't want to take her up on it.

"That's kind of you," she finally said.

"I guess I'll just put my request in and say I'd appreciate it if you don't take six years, or even six months really." He didn't want to narrow her down to a specific time frame and push her further and faster than she wanted to go, but he really didn't want to spend years sleeping apart while she got to know him.

"Sure. I can promise you that."

"Do you have any idea how long it's going to take?" He shouldn't have asked that question. That was his more selfish part coming out. Because it let her know that he was hoping for more and fast.

"Not long. I don't think it would take a month?" She looked a little worried, like she was concerned that her answer was going to be longer than he wanted. But it really wasn't up to him.

"That's fine. Why do you look worried?"

"I didn't want to be unreasonable. And I wasn't sure what unreasonable is in this case."

"As long as you're going with your gut, I don't think it's unreasonable, although I do think it's a bad idea to live by your feelings. My mom always said that, and I think she's right. We have a tendency to do what we feel like doing and not what we know we should. Although, you just showed me that you're willing to correct yourself when you're doing something opposite as to what you know you should. I liked seeing that."

"Thanks. I hope that's typical of my personality. I've lived by myself for a while, and I'm used to calling the shots. This is going to be an adjustment for me."

"And for me too. I've lived by myself for a long time as well, or at the very least, been in charge of myself for a long time, and I'm not used to thinking about other people. But that was one of the things that I talked to the Lord about this morning, being considerate and unselfish. That is definitely an area I need to work on. Especially with you."

Her hand slipped off his, and it made him sad to feel it go, but they smiled at each other, and he got the feeling that they were in agreement over pretty much everything. And the things that they didn't agree on weren't that important. Or maybe they were just things they could compromise about.

Still, he had figured out from their conversation that Cassie thought a lot differently than what he did, and he knew just the person he could talk to to help him out. Someone who wouldn't blab to everyone else and who loved him as much as a person could love another person.

"If you're okay, I'm going to go out to the ranch for the night. I'll see to the stock in the morning, and then...I'll come back in?"

She nodded.

"I'll try calling the lawyer again, and I'll let you know what he says when I get here."

"That sounds good."

"All right. You go on to bed. I'll turn off the lights and lock the door behind me. Okay?"

She smiled a little, and he remembered that she was used to taking care of herself. But he couldn't help it, he couldn't just walk out the door while she was still sitting there and not know that she was safely tucked in her bed, with the door locked. After all, she was his wife, and he was going to take care of her. Even if he did bumble his way through their relationship.

Chapter 12

Lark Stryker rolled over and looked at the clock.

Five AM.

That meant she'd been in bed for two hours. Mr. Connelly, a gentleman farmer who had horses and lived an hour and a half away from Sweet Water, had called her out to his farm yesterday for his mare who was having trouble during labor.

It turned out his mare was carrying twins, and Lark ended up delivering them both by C-section.

She had stayed, trying to coax life into the two little ones and hoping the mom would snap out of the anesthetic and come around.

When she left at three AM, all three of them were doing what she would consider okay. Not good, not great, but they weren't dead. So they were okay.

She planned to go back out today, but some confounding knocking had woken her up way too early.

Just as she thought about it, it came again.

Hurrying out of bed, realizing she had fallen across the covers without even taking her clothes off, she grabbed a hair tie from the dresser where she'd thrown it as she took her ponytail out when she'd stumbled into her room, and hurried down the stairs.

Mabel, her assistant who was still in vet school, and three other girls lived in the house with her. She didn't want them to wake up. If this was an animal emergency, she would handle it.

The pounding stopped when she turned the kitchen light on, and she hurried to the door, throwing it open.

"You should look to see who it is before you just open your door to anyone, especially at this time of night."

Mav, her youngest brother and her favorite, stood on her porch, a grin on his face and a twinkle in his eye. He looked like the same old Mav. But she had heard something about him yesterday.

"Did you get married yesterday?" she asked, pretty sure that's what she had heard, but it was pretty early and she hadn't had much sleep.

"Sure did, Sis. I didn't see you at my wedding, come to think of it."

"I wasn't invited."

"No one else was invited, either, but that didn't stop them from showing up. Didn't stop the whole town from showing up."

She shook her head. "You're going to have to tell me about it, but I need a cup of coffee."

"I thought you'd be up. It's five o'clock."

She jerked her head, indicating that he could come in, and she walked over to the coffee maker. "I was up until three delivering foals. I thought I'd give myself a little bit of time to sleep."

"I guess you deserve it after that. Everybody make it?"

"As far as I know. I was going to drive over and see about them this morning."

"Couldn't you just call?"

"I guess I could call. Still, I told him I'd be there to check, so that's what I'm going to do." She started the coffee maker and leaned back against the counter, her arms crossed over her chest. "As soon as I have some coffee in hand, we'll need to go outside. I don't want to wake Mabel and the girls."

"How many girls do you have living with you right now?"

"There are three of them. One just went home."

Mav nodded, but he didn't ask anything else. She really might not be able to answer. People asked her where the girls came from, and she didn't even really know.

People just talked. Someone had a daughter who was having trouble, and talked to a friend who talked to a friend who talked to a grandmother who talked to a Sunday school teacher who knew of Lark, and they sent them here.

Lark had enough work to keep a whole trove of people busy, and a lot of times, that's just what people needed. Something to make them feel worthwhile. Something to give them purpose in their life. Something to keep their mind off their troubles and off themselves and focus on something else, caring for something else. Giving their attention and their love to something else.

Once a person did that, it often made their troubles go away. Or they seemed much smaller.

Lark had had some success in that area, but it wasn't something she sought out. It was just when God opened the door and sent someone to her, either via a telephone call or a visit, asking if she could take a girl, she just never said no. It was her policy that if God asked, she said yes.

It hadn't always been easy, but it had always been rewarding.

She turned to pour herself a cup of coffee, thinking about her younger self and how she had just wanted one thing. To marry the man she loved. And he hadn't wanted to have anything to do with her.

She'd actually begged him. And he said no. Told her that she needed to grow up of all things, told her that he wasn't the slightest bit interested and that she should stop wasting her time on a dairy farm that was slowly sinking into bankruptcy, and to go to school and get an education so she could get a real job and have a real life.

She hadn't wanted to believe him when he said he wasn't interested in her, but she eventually had come to admit that he had never given her any indication he was. It had always been her chasing after him.

Still, she hadn't had any plans to go to school until an anonymous benefactor had paid for all eight years of her education.

She had never been successful in figuring out who it was, but she would love to thank him or her.

Regardless, she wasn't the kind of woman who fell in love easily, and if she were being honest, she still had feelings for the dairy farmer. Even though he was a lot older than she was. Almost two decades.

She swallowed, turning away from the counter, two cups of coffee in her hands. "Do you still take yours black?"

"I drink it however I have to, even if it tastes like candy. Especially this time of morning."

"I bet you didn't get much more sleep than I did. But you could always run on less."

"Four hours is pretty much all I need. And yeah, that's almost what I got last night. Not quite." He took a cup from her, and then he walked to the door, opening it for her.

She appreciated that he remembered that she hadn't wanted to stay inside and wake the girls.

They would sleep until at least six if she let them.

That meant she had forty-five minutes or so to talk to her brother. Which she would cherish, since she didn't get to see him nearly as much as she would like to. They were both busy. And Mav didn't stay in one place for very long.

"Are you going to tell me about this marriage of yours?" she asked, figuring that must have something to do with the reason he was there.

Why he wasn't at home, snuggled up in bed with his wife, would surely come out in their conversation. Although, she hadn't even known he had a girlfriend. So, when she heard that he'd gotten married, she'd been rather shocked.

"I got a letter."

Lark's head jerked up. She had heard about the letters. Had gotten one herself, but there was only one man she wanted to marry, and he had told her no. She had mentioned the money to him, and when he turned her down, not even wanting her if she came with a billion dollars, she'd ripped the letter up and thrown it away.

"Was there a one billion dollars offer in it?" she asked, tentatively, because it would sound outrageous to anyone who had not gotten one.

"How did you know?"

"I had one myself."

"You need to hurry up and get married, sis. Before it expires."

She shook her head. "It expired years ago. Back when I was just eighteen."

"Someone wanted you to get married when you were eighteen?"

"Maybe they knew me better than I did. But I didn't. And I tore the letter up and threw it away."

"You ripped up a letter that offered you one billion dollars?"

"Sure. What's one billion dollars when you have to marry someone you don't want to marry?"

"It's one billion dollars," Mav said, like he couldn't believe that she could turn that down.

"Are you gonna tell me you married some random person just to get money?" she asked, trying not to sound quite as scandalized as she felt. Which was really scandalized. And upset.

Mav looked sheepish.

"You did!" she said, trying not to sound accusatory but knowing that she did. "You married someone you don't love, you don't know...just some random person to get money? I can't believe it!"

"Hey. Don't knock it." He didn't seem to be able to think of anything else to say. He shifted and took a gulp of the hot coffee. "I have a question about her."

"Who was it?" she asked, figuring he had found the absolute biggest gold digger in town to hitch up with. Knowing Mav, who had no common sense at times, he wouldn't care that she had no character and no morals, and he would have just hitched himself to her anyway.

"Cassie Rowe," Mav said.

Lark gasped. She knew Cassie. She stuttered. "But she's a nice girl."

"I know," Mav said, with more feeling than she would have expected out of him.

"What do you mean you know?" she asked, instantly suspicious.

"I know she's nice. She was nice to me, and when no one else in town would have me, she stepped out of the pew and stepped up beside me." Briefly he told her about being alone, with no one wanting him all day, until Cassie finally stepped out.

"Wow. I can't believe she did that."

"I couldn't either. But I read something on her phone that I wanted to ask you about."

"What was that?" she asked, curious.

"It said 'congratulations on marrying the guy you always had a crush on.' Or something like that. Basically, it insinuated that she's liked me all of her life."

"I see." Lark pressed her lips together. She had heard that. Had heard that Cassie had had a huge crush on Mav. It was a couple of years ago, and she thought it would have just been a passing fancy. After all, Mav wasn't exactly known for his ability to attract women and keep them. They seemed to flock to him and then flocked away just as fast.

"Do you know if that's true?" Mav pushed when she didn't say anything.

Should she admit it? Would that be in Cassie's best interest? She didn't want to do something that would end up hurting Cassie. Or she didn't want to make Mav arrogant and conceited about the woman who had chosen to marry him. He might crush her, if he thought that he had her in the bank.

"Lark. You know something you're not telling me."

"I don't want you to take advantage of her. I'm not sure if telling you is going to be the best thing for you. Or especially for her."

"It will be. I promise. I...I was actually here because I wanted to ask your advice on being married."

"Me?" she gasped. "I'm not married. What makes you think I can give you advice?"

"Because of the girls you have. You see it all. I know it's not a marriage thing, but you know what they need. You know what makes people tick."

"No. I know what makes *animals* tick."

"You're observant, and you pay attention to things. I know you can tell me the things that I need to improve. What I need to do in order to have a marriage that lasts with my wife. I don't want to be a statistic. I don't want to be divorced. I don't want this to be a big mistake. I want to make it work. And you were the only person that I could think of that I could ask who wouldn't make fun of me and think I was just goofing off like I always do. I need you to take me seriously and give me good answers."

"All right." She was honored that he had come to her. That he thought that she would give him good advice. Of course she was going to take him seriously. She always did. Even when other people just dismissed him as a big goof-off, she'd known that there was a serious man there, one that just needed a little bit of time to grow up.

She believed in him.

"Maybe because you just said all of that, I will say that I heard a year or two ago that Cassie had a huge crush on you. That she'd liked you for years and years. I think it was about the time that Katie and Flynn Powers got married."

"Yeah. Miss Charlene actually pulled me aside to help her and told me to just act like myself. She said she didn't think that Katie would choose me, but she wanted me to be willing. I played along, and it worked out the way she thought it was going to."

"Yeah. I think it was about that time that I heard that Katie found out Cassie had a crush on you, and she wouldn't choose you, because she didn't want to hurt her friend."

"Really?"

"That's what I heard. I can't guarantee that's accurate, but it sounds about right to me. I know Katie would have done that, and the person that I heard it from wouldn't lie to me. But please don't use that against her. She...she's pretty calm and contained, but I think sometimes people like that get hurt a lot easier when they finally do let their guard down, because they do it so rarely."

He nodded. "I'm not going to hurt her on purpose. But I need advice from you. She thinks so much differently than I do. I don't know when I open my mouth if I'm going to offend or upset her until the words are out and I see her face show expression, and then I know I shouldn't have said it, but I don't always know what I said wrong."

"I'm probably not going to be able to help you with that. That's part of what the Bible means when it says that a man is supposed to dwell with his wife according to knowledge. You're going to have to learn about her. Figure her out. Do the things you know she likes and not do the things you know she doesn't. That's on you."

"Sometimes being a man really stinks."

Mav sounded so disgusted that Lark had to laugh.

"It's not that bad," she said, humor lacing every word.

"Too much responsibility. I just want to be a kid."

"No. You don't want that. You want to grow up. You want to have a lifetime of accomplishments behind you, striking out into the unknown, conquering things. Having the legacy of a family who loves the Lord following after you. You want that. And you have to work for it. Those things don't come easily. The things that matter."

"I know you're right. I just... Sometimes the work feels too hard."

"But it's fun too. Being married is fun." Lark looked down, trying to get her face in his line of vision so he would meet her eyes. She set her coffee cup on the banister and took him by the arms, waiting until he met her eyes and she could see his face in the glow of the rising sun.

"Marriage is fun. Laughter should be the soundtrack of your marriage. Make it fun, Mav. That's one of your fortes. She had a crush on you, I guarantee you she loved your sense of humor. She loved the way you make people laugh. She loved that you're goofy and that you don't take everything seriously. I promise you, she couldn't possibly have had a crush on you and not love that about you. She doesn't want you to be a stodgy old man."

"Thank God. Because she's never going to get that," Mav said, but some of the frustration and tension drained out of him.

"Just give her attention. Look at her. Truly see her. Pay attention to what she likes. If she says that she's taking her shoes off and wearing socks around the house because she loves her big fluffy socks, get her a pair of big fluffy socks the next time you're in town. Show her that you listen. Don't forget her special days—her birthday, for goodness' sake. Find out when it is, and then set eleven alarms on your phone if you have to. It's not about getting her a gift, it's about paying attention and not forgetting about her. Because forgetting equals not caring."

"That stinks. Because I'm terrible at remembering anything. I don't even remember my own birthday."

"I don't believe that," Lark said, rolling her eyes, and Mav grinned guiltily. "Pay attention to her. Know her. And then put her first. Before yourself."

"I guess that was one of the things I wanted to tell you. I kinda figured out that that was something that I was doing wrong. I knew that I wasn't doing a very good job of doing anything but living my life for me. And yesterday, before all of the marriage stuff went down, I told the Lord if He got me out of the pit I was in with my farm, then I would live my life for Him. I've made promises to Him before that I haven't kept, but He didn't give up on me, and He kept His end of the bargain, showing me the letter, which I had totally misplaced for years. I hadn't even opened it. And part of what I knew I had been doing wrong was being selfish."

It didn't surprise her at all that he hadn't opened it. What surprised her was that he'd opened it in time. But then, God's timing was always right.

"Then you're halfway there. Recognizing that you have a problem is a big part of solving it. But you have to think about her. And put her first. I know Cassie, and I'm almost positive that you're not going to have to worry about her thinking about herself over you."

Mav seemed to be thinking about something, and then he said softly, "She's already put me first. All day yesterday. Not just by stepping out, but she hadn't wanted to share a bedroom, and then she realized that she wasn't letting me be the leader of the house by telling me what we were going to do, so she changed her mind and said that we could if I wanted to."

Lark blinked, stepping back. That was huge. And very big on Cassie's part. Brave too.

"What did you do?" she asked, hoping that her brother hadn't taken Cassie up on that offer. That he'd realized that they probably really did need time to learn about each other and to know each other and to make Cassie feel comfortable. That a little bit of the foundation would be so much better than stepping into things they weren't ready for.

"I told her that I wasn't going to share a room with her until she was ready and basically delegated the decision to her. Acknowledging that I was in charge but giving her the responsibility in that area."

"Well, Mav. I never thought I would call you romantic, but that was very romantic." Lark put a hand over her heart and fluttered, just to be goofy, and he laughed at her.

"Oh, stop. You're going to give me a big head."

"I'm gonna start looking for my little brother, because I can hardly believe that you're him."

"Well, between God and marriage, I had a lot of opportunity to grow up yesterday. I don't think anybody can do it on the spur of the moment and in one day, but I think, for the first time in my life, I'm headed in the right direction."

"You'll have to talk to Mom. She'll be so proud of you."

"I plan to. You think it will make her happy?"

"I know it will."

He blew out a breath. "I'm sorry I got you up so early. I didn't realize you were up so late last night. And now you probably won't get to bed until this evening."

"It's okay. It's part of my job. And some days I don't have anything to do, so there's that."

"I bet those days are few and far between."

"They are. But they make me happy that I have a job, a calling, and I feel useful and needed in my life. That's important."

"Thanks for talking to me. I appreciate it. I really appreciate your advice. If you think of anything else, you can always text me. I'm open to all ideas."

"I'll do that. And if you have any questions, you know you can always text me, but do remember that I'm your one sibling that isn't married. So you might be better off talking to your married siblings, rather than coming to your one single sibling for marriage advice."

"I think you gave me some good ideas. I don't regret coming. But if my marriage doesn't work out, it's all your fault."

"Seriously, Mav?" she laughed.

"All right. Thanks for the coffee," he said, draining the last of his cup, giving her a one-armed hug with the hand that wasn't holding his coffee, and then handing her his mug before he waved and stepped off the porch.

She watched him go, happy but a little bit sad. She was the last remaining sibling that wasn't married.

Lark sighed. Not regretting her decision so long ago, that if her farmer wouldn't have her, she wouldn't marry anyone. But sometimes she was lonely.

Lord, You know. I don't even know what to ask, just help me, please.

Her farmer didn't live that far away. But the last she heard, he had a woman living with him. And while he had animals, he never called her out to his farm. She could only assume that that meant he didn't want her there.

Plus, if he did have a woman living with him, she didn't want him anyway. She just wanted the image of him that she had in her head.

The man she fell in love with.

Dumping the rest of her coffee out in the flower bed, she turned and walked back into the house.

Chapter 13

T he sun shone in on Cassie as she lay in bed with her eyes closed in that fuzzy land between fully sleeping and fully waking.

She could feel Phyllis snuggled up beside her, snoring softly, sound asleep.

Phyllis wouldn't wake up until Cassie got up.

Phyllis was not a morning dog.

Cassie smiled a little to herself and shifted slightly, curling her legs up and tucking her hands under her chin, feeling the sun on her face, but still not wanting to wake up.

She'd been having the nicest dream. A dream where Mav asked her to marry him, declared his undying love, and wanted to spend his life with her.

It wasn't a dream she allowed herself to think about, not since she'd promised the Lord she wouldn't, but it was one that she had previously.

She always woke up feeling slightly discontented after it, because it felt impossible.

But today...

Her eyes shot open.

Had yesterday actually happened?

Had she married Mav?

She pulled her hands out from underneath her chin and looked at them.

No rings. It was a little disappointing. She furrowed her brows and tried to think. Had she really been waiting at the church? It had been late. She didn't usually stay up that late. But she was pretty sure Mav was looking for a wife. She had heard that at the feed store. She remembered seeing his brother's surprise. That was real.

But had she stepped down the aisle and walked down to the front with him? Had he sat at her kitchen table?

He drank coffee. She'd given him coffee. If he'd actually been at her kitchen table, it was possible she might still smell him, because he had a unique scent that she felt like she would recognize anywhere now that she'd smelled it up close, but more concrete than that, there would be two dirty coffee cups in her sink. Because her dishes had been done, but she distinctly remembered putting two coffee cups in the sink.

She got out of bed so quickly she accidentally kicked Phyllis off.

The dog whimpered, then got up and stretched, forgiving Cassie instantly for her inconsideration.

That was the nice thing about dogs, they didn't hold grudges.

"I'm sorry, sweetie. But I'm in a rush. Was Mav really here last night?"

The dog didn't tell her, of course, but she wagged her tail and licked Cassie's toes as she bent down to scratch between the floppy ears.

"I think he was. I think... I think I'm actually married. I think we talked about where we're going to sleep, and he turned me down when I finally invited him to sleep with me. Figures."

Phyllis never answered her. Cassie was among the seventy percent of Americans who talked to their pets.

She couldn't imagine being among the thirty percent who didn't. People liked their dogs but didn't talk to them? How did they interact with their animals they didn't talk to?

That didn't matter. Mav was one who mattered. Marriage was the thing that mattered. Was she really supposed to be packing up her house and getting ready to move into his house? Had they talked about that?

She tried to think back. Think about any plans that they had made today, but she couldn't really remember anything... Maybe something about a lawyer. He was going to try to call the lawyer.

One billion dollars.

He had said that they were going to get one billion dollars.

That was when she knew that as real as everything felt, it was actually a dream.

She stopped rushing to put clothes on, realizing that she put her shirt on backwards and was putting a leg in the wrong side of her pants.

Stupid.

She pulled her pants back off, took the shirt off, flipped it around, stuck that on, and decided to go with a skirt. That way, if she got it wrong, it wouldn't matter.

After she shoved her feet in her flip-flops, she scooped Phyllis up from the floor and padded down the hall.

Too bad it wasn't real. It was a really nice dream. And so very real.

She almost could imagine Mav had kissed her cheek after the wedding.

Okay, that seemed a little real, because if it had been a dream, he wouldn't have kissed her cheek. Even if it was her fault. It would have definitely have been a much deeper, more real, more intimate kiss.

For sure.

Sighing, figuring she wasn't the only one who had dreams that she wished were real, she walked into the kitchen, intending to go out the back door to let Phyllis loose in the backyard.

But there was a man at her table.

She stopped short in the doorway, clutching Phyllis to her chest.

The man had one ankle resting on top of the other knee, his fingers drumming on the table. His eyes were glued on the doorway, and when she stopped, her eyes flew to his, and they met.

Maybe it wasn't a dream.

Because Mav Stryker was sitting in her kitchen.

"Hello?" she said, half expecting him to disappear in a puff of smoke.

Maybe her cancer was back. Maybe she had a brain tumor this time.

If this was what brain tumors were like, she wouldn't mind having a brain tumor. She smiled at the thought, even as the man said, "Good morning. Sleep well?"

"Mav?" she said, still not believing that he was really in her kitchen, unwilling to keep Phyllis waiting while she talked to an apparition. She walked slowly toward him until she passed him.

"You look like you don't really know me. Did you forget that we got married last night?"

"So that wasn't a dream," she mumbled to herself with her hand on the doorknob. "Did we really get married?"

"I feel like you might have been imbibing alcohol, though I didn't smell it on your breath during the ceremony. But you're kind of acting like you're hung over."

Hung over with happiness? She rolled her eyes at the thought. Opening the door, she set Phyllis down, knowing that she would be safe in the fenced backyard. Normally she walked out with her, just looking at the day, enjoying the weather and being outside, before she came in and got started on her work.

But not today.

Mav was at her table.

Mav was at her table!

She threw a hand up to her throat. Mav was at her table. What was she doing walking by, leaving him alone, mumbling nonsense about dreams and ignoring him? Here she was, the first day of married life, married to the man she never thought she'd have, and she basically walked by him like he wasn't even there. Like she didn't believe he was real.

In her defense, it was because she didn't believe he was real, but still.

She walked back, stopping beside him. He dropped his foot to the floor and straightened a little, resting both hands in his lap, as he looked over his shoulder at her, following her with his eyes and head until she stood beside him.

"Sorry. I guess I am a little loopy this morning. I woke up thinking that that couldn't possibly be real. First of all, because it's you, and second because I remembered something about one billion dollars, which is obviously the stuff of dreams and not reality. But also, it was pretty late. Way past my bedtime."

"Really? I never go to bed before midnight."

"I'm never up after midnight. In fact, I'm not usually up after nine o'clock."

"Hmm. That might get interesting."

"We can compromise. Ten thirty?"

He laughed. "Maybe we can find something to do from nine o'clock until midnight that involves us being in bed but not actually sleeping."

She knew exactly what he was saying, but she said, "You like to read in bed too? Sweet."

He snorted, and she said, "Would you like coffee? I feel like I really need it this morning."

"I've already had three cups, but I think I can safely drink three more until I need to call it quits."

"Wow. I cannot handle that much coffee. One cup is pretty much my limit."

"I would suggest a compromise for this too, but I didn't like the way the last one panned out."

"So you don't like to read?"

"I don't, but that wasn't what I was thinking."

"I know."

He laughed. "I thought you were messing with me."

"I'm allowed, right?"

"I like it."

His tone of voice said that he actually did. Which surprised her. Sometimes when people were used to picking on other people, they didn't like to be picked on themselves. But from what she'd heard and observed, Mav could take it as well as he dished it out.

"What are you planning on doing today?" he asked. "I don't think we hashed that out, unless you had a dream that I didn't?"

"Are you making fun of me?"

"You did come down here kind of looking at me like you didn't expect me to be in your kitchen. I *am* your husband."

"I know. It just takes a lot of getting used to."

"You need to get used to it. Because I'm here."

"All right. I know."

"Did you have plans for today?"

"I really didn't have anything in particular I was doing. We talked a little bit last night, but not really about what we're going to do." She had that project she had to work on, but she didn't want to lose spending time with Mav, if he was actually going to spend time with her today, by saying that she had to work. She'd get it done by the end of the week.

Plus, they weren't taking a honeymoon, so surely she could take one day off and spend it with him.

"I've called the lawyer twice, and he hasn't answered, so I wanted to drive out to see him."

"Drive to the lawyer's?"

"Yeah. I was hoping you'd go with me." He didn't sound like he was totally confident about asking that, like she might actually turn him down. As if.

"Sure. Is that normal? For people to go to the lawyer's to see if they're a legit business?"

"I don't know. But he's not answering his phone, so I'm gonna go see for myself."

"All right. Where is he, in Rockerton?"

Mav puffed out a breath. "No. Not exactly. He's actually quite a distance away. I think I figured it would take us an hour and a half to drive there. Maybe two. I hope you don't mind that long of a drive?"

"No. Not at all." Actually, she was looking forward to it. A whole three or four hours to spend with Mav. To get to know him, talk to him. If he'd talk to her. She supposed he might be the kind of person who turned the radio on and never said anything else to the people who were sitting in the car with him.

She could handle it if that was the kind of person he was, but it would be a little bit disappointing. She'd rather stay home and work.

"All right. And then, I guess we never talked about what we were going to do. I mean, you're in charge of the bedroom and when we decide to share, and we talked about where we're going to live, but I wasn't sure how you felt about it."

"I guess where we live is your decision, isn't it?"

"Well, I don't want to be the kind of person who makes decisions without consulting with you."

"I appreciate that." She smiled, handing him the coffee she had made. She'd noticed over the years that he drank it black, so that's how she handed it to him now.

"Thank you."

"My pleasure," she said, setting her cup down, then pulling out a chair and sitting down catty-corner from him. "I assume you had animals to attend to this morning?"

"I did."

"You can hardly keep them here, and I wouldn't want you to have to get up every morning and ride out to the farm to do that. All I have is Phyllis, and she'll be happy anywhere."

"I take it you have a fenced yard?" Mav asked, looking at the door.

"I do."

"I don't. So if that's what Phyllis is used to, we might have to make one for her."

She wanted to put her hand over her heart, but she didn't. Still, she got up and walked over to the door, not because she thought Phyllis was ready to come in, but because she couldn't believe that he was being so thoughtful. He would actually make a fenced yard for Phyllis? He had realized that was important to her?

She didn't want him to be like that. And almost resented it. She already was half in love with him, and if he was considerate, not only just of her, but of her dog as well, she was hopeless.

She would be falling in love with him, and that scared her. Because he would have the power to hurt her.

Chapter 14

"Are you hungry? I can make breakfast before we go?" she asked, loving the idea that Mav was here, talking to her, and they were spending time alone together.

"I can help. I can make eggs and toast. Although, I can't make eggs over easy."

"That's fine. I don't like runny eggs anyway. And I think I have some bacon I can fry, too."

"You talked me into it."

She laughed, getting up and walking to the refrigerator, conscious of him standing behind her. He seemed to fill her kitchen with his presence, which wasn't a bad feeling. Actually, she liked it.

Loved it, more like it. Just having him there. Having him doing something with her. She probably should explain to him that this was part of building a relationship, but she didn't want to dredge up the conversation of last night. She just wanted to enjoy the moment.

"We didn't really get a honeymoon. Maybe I should take us out for breakfast?" Mav asked, but Cassie shook her head.

"Unless you really want to. I'm just as happy here, with just us. As long as you're doing it with me."

He stopped, with his hand on the bread bag. And looked at her. "Building a relationship?"

"Yes. I didn't want to say anything, but yes."

"You really think that us being in the kitchen together is a good thing?"

"Sure. Why not?"

"Because it's kind of boring. I mean, we're just cooking. It's breakfast. We're not even cooking anything fun."

Her face fell a little bit, and her heart kind of trembled. "Do we have to be doing something bigger or 'fun' together in order for you to enjoy being with me?" She didn't really want to ask that question. Maybe he wouldn't answer it or even know how to answer it. Because it probably wasn't something he thought about.

"No. I... I guess we haven't spent a lot of time together, but all the time I've spent with you has been good. It's not like I'm looking for an excuse to get away from you."

"That's a relief. I probably will never be the most entertaining person in the room, so if you're looking for someone who's an entertainer, you picked the wrong person."

"I guess I have enough actor in me for both of us. Someone said you'd be good for me because you would ground me. Maybe I'll be good for you because I'll get you out of your comfort zone a little bit."

"Starting today, because it's not exactly comfortable to walk into my kitchen and see a man there, although I liked it," she added quickly, lest he think that she didn't. "And I wouldn't be traveling to a lawyer's office this morning either, so you're definitely pulling me out of my comfort zone. And I like it."

"It's a good thing." He stuck two pieces of bread in the toaster while she cut four pieces of bacon in half and set them in the frying pan.

They didn't say anything for a bit until she had the eggs in a bowl, scrambling them with a fork, and he, leaning against the counter, one foot crossed over the other, his arms crossed, waited for the toast to pop up.

He said, "So, if the billion dollars is legit, what do you want to do with it?"

"It's not really mine, is it?"

"All right, maybe we should have a different conversation. We're married, so whatever is mine is yours, and I'm going to assume whatever is yours is mine. It's not going to be this is mine and this is yours, right?"

"I think you're right. When God joined us together, he said we'd become one. So, that means there really isn't mine and yours, there's just ours."

"Speaking of, I totally forgot that we need to go to the courthouse and get a license."

"I forgot that too." She laughed, unable to believe she had forgotten something so basic.

"You really did think it was a dream this morning, me sitting in your kitchen?"

"I sure did. I had a hard time waking up this morning. I liked the dream."

"I get the feeling that real life hasn't been that good for you."

"No. But a lot of times, life is how you look at it and what make it out to be, you know?"

"I know. But sometimes we get things handed to us that really aren't fair or right, and it's hard to put a good spin on them."

"I'll not argue with that. Because you're right. But still, it really is all in how we look at it. And what we think we're going to get out of it. If we focus on the negative, and on the bad, and all the terrible things... If I did anyway, I'd be a pretty unhappy person."

"Yet you can't believe it when good things happen. If you can call getting married to me a good thing."

"It's a good thing. It really is." She could feel her cheeks heating, and she concentrated a little more on the eggs in the skillet than what was strictly necessary. She didn't want him to see her reaction, because she really did think being married to him was a good thing. Far better than what he probably thought being married to her was.

"I guess I was just thinking that is why you had trouble believing that what happened to you is real. Because you really wanted it to happen, and there haven't been a whole lot of those things happening to you in your life."

"You're right."

"But a billion dollars would be a good thing, right?"

"I think so. As long as we're wise about it. I think sometimes money ruins people. Does that make sense?"

"I suppose. Maybe I'm just not mature enough to think it's going to happen to me, because I kind of feel like it's like ninety-seven percent good."

"I think it could go either way. Honestly. And that's not taking a negative view, that's just looking at how money has affected other people."

"Like celebrities?"

"Yeah. Although, fame affects celebrities in negative ways, too, I think. We get used to people thinking that we're really something, and we start to believe that we are or start to act like we are anyway, and really, whatever it is that we've done that made us famous isn't anything that we could have done without God's favor and His hand in our life. We want to take the credit for ourselves, and that goes to our head. I think it can be addicting too."

"I agree with that. That fame, or people telling you how wonderful you are, can be addicting. You want to hear it from more and more people, and you leave the people behind who like you for who you actually are, instead of who they think you are."

"And God gets left behind as well."

"Yeah. I suppose a lot of money makes you start to feel like you don't really need the Lord. All right. You convinced me. I can see how things that we typically see as good things could end up being really bad."

The toast popped up, and he pulled it out, sticking two more pieces in before he started to butter it.

"I like a lot of butter on mine, like it melted until the bread is crunchy on the bottom and soft on the top. How do you like it?"

"Not like that. That sounds like a gluey mess."

"Mmm. It's a buttery mess. A really good one."

"All right. I've noted it, and I'll not tell you how to make toast for yourself, but for me, just a tiny little bit of butter. I like my toast to be crunchy. So not too much."

"Got it. I'll do my best to make it just the way you like it."

"Bacon crispy or just cooked?" she asked, since they were getting to know each other. Which was a fun way to do it, as they were actually making things.

"Crispy. For sure."

"Goodness. I think we're opposite in everything. Because I like mine just cooked, but still soft."

"Yuck. That doesn't sound good."

"Oh, it's the best."

"You said you don't like your eggs runny, right?"

She smiled. He was listening to her, and it warmed her heart. "Nope, definitely not. No one likes that. Do they?"

"I think it's a thing. I don't know anyone who does, but since we're opposites in everything, I figured that you'd probably like them that way."

"No. I like mine best with mushrooms and onions and spinach and a lot of cheese, but I don't usually have them like that, because I always end up adding more ingredients than I have eggs, and I end up with a mess."

"I like my eggs with salsa. Which I suppose is kind of the same thing, since there's onions at least in it."

"I actually have some salsa in the refrigerator, so I'm glad you said something."

She flipped the eggs, then walked to the refrigerator and pulled out the salsa.

The rest of their meal went similarly, with them talking about their likes and dislikes, and by the time they cleaned up the dishes and washed them, with her saying she preferred to wash, and him saying he preferred to dry, which was the one thing where their opposite tendencies actually complemented each other, she felt like she was getting to know him. The real him, not the guy that she crushed on all the time. That guy was still there, but she was realizing that there was a real man underneath the perception that she had of him. A real man who she was discovering she liked very much.

They drove to Rockerton and to the courthouse, got the license, and went back and visited the pastor and took care of everything that they needed to. So it was almost eleven o'clock before they were on their way to see the lawyer.

Mav had tried to call him before they'd left, and he still hadn't answered. Which didn't exactly surprise Cassie. She had decided he must be on vacation, and if it was just him manning the office, it would be closed down until he came back.

So, when they pulled into a place that looked more like a petting zoo than an attorney's office, she was a little discombobulated.

She had figured he was a single attorney, working for himself. The petting zoo should not have been a surprise because Mav had warned her about it. It still seemed odd.

"Are you sure this is the right place?" she asked, even though they had checked the address on the GPS, and it had taken them right to the parking lot.

"This is what it said. And when I talked to my stepdad, he said that the man had a petting zoo. I... I guess I wasn't picturing the law office and the petting zoo being in the same place."

"Yeah. I don't think I would have ever pictured that either."

Mav, his hand still on the steering wheel, stared at the small building that looked more like a train station at an amusement park and not something that would actually house a lawyer's office. "I guess we won't know unless we go and check it out."

She was glad he was with her. She probably wouldn't have gone in. She would have just decided that she was crazy and left.

"You good with that?" he asked as he put a hand on the door latch.

"Yes. I appreciate you being here. I was just thinking that without you, I probably would have left."

"Just another area where we seem to be opposite," he said, and she knew that Mav was anything but shy and retiring.

They laughed together before they got out of the pickup, meeting in front of it with Mav grabbing her hand.

She almost stopped in her tracks when his fingers closed around hers.

She was not expecting it. He had taken her hand some of the other places they'd been, including in front of the preacher, and she wouldn't have said she didn't like it. But it was knowing him better, talking to him and feeling closer that made it feel so much...different, better, and it made her smile. She looked over at him to find him looking down at her.

"I like that," she said, like he couldn't tell from the grin on her face.

"I like it too." He sounded a little bit more surprised, like he hadn't been expecting to enjoy walking hand in hand with someone. Or maybe he hadn't thought about it. She supposed the second was probably true. Mav seemed to have only certain things he thought about, especially when it came to relationships, and she got the feeling that the small pleasure of walking hand in hand with someone was something that he hadn't considered.

There was some confusion as they walked to the building, trying to figure out where they were supposed to go, when a small, slightly bald man popped up from behind the counter.

"I'm Peregrine Czeitzler. Are you here to visit the petting zoo?" he asked, sounding hopeful.

"No. Actually we're here to see an attorney. We have some business to take care of with him."

The man's face fell, his eyes behind the little spectacles that he wore dipping downward for just a moment, before he perked up, only half as excited as he looked before.

"I see. I would like to say that any lawyer's fees you incur are halved when you also purchase a ticket to the petting zoo."

"Uh, okay?" Mav said. Then he said, "We'll take two tickets."

Cassie didn't mean to, but her hand tightened in his, and her body jerked. She didn't want to go to the petting zoo.

"Are you okay?" Mav asked, looking down at her in concern.

She forced herself to nod, and he looked back at the man, completing the transaction while she gave herself a little lecture.

She needed to remember that her default answer didn't have to be no all the time. There was no harm in going to the petting zoo. There was no harm in buying tickets. Even if there wasn't one billion dollars, the twenty bucks that Mav had to spend was not going to break them, and it would not hurt her at all to go in and see animals.

Why did she always say no? It was like an automatic reaction for her.

She had to break herself of it. After all, she guessed that Mav probably said yes more often than he said no. And most of the time, either answer could be correct.

Chapter 15

"All right," said the little man, after he wrote the receipt by hand and handed the tickets to them. "You can enter right through that door and just follow the walk. It will take you around, bringing you out over there. That's where my lawyer's office is." The man pointed behind him, across the three feet to the counter and the door that was right beside it.

"Can we do the attorney obligations before we do the petting zoo?" Mav asked slowly, as though the man had taken him aback. He'd certainly surprised Cassie.

"You can, but the door will lead you right to the lawyer's office, so since you have the tickets, you should do the petting zoo first."

"All right. We'll do the petting zoo first," Mav said, sounding like it wasn't his first choice, but he wasn't going to argue.

He shoved his wallet back in his pocket and took her hand again.

She loved that he didn't grab it exactly but slid their fingers together, almost as though he liked that feeling as well.

It made her smile every time. Which was silly and such a newlywed thing to do. She supposed by the time they'd been married for a year or two, holding hands would be so old hat they probably wouldn't even do it anymore, but she loved it. It made her feel connected to him in a way that talking didn't. It was like she needed that touch to have the connection.

Mav might not understand, maybe he would get tired of holding her hand, so she would enjoy it for as long as it lasted.

"After you," Mav said as he opened the gate for her, indicating she could walk through first.

She clutched his hand, and if he noticed and thought it was odd, he didn't say.

It wasn't that she was always scared of new places and new things, but... It was just that she wasn't used to them. She'd spent so much of her youth in hospitals, and she'd grown comfortable in those, but she'd never been to a petting zoo.

"As petting zoos go, this one's a little bit different," Mav said, looking around.

"I wouldn't know."

He stopped. "You've never been to a petting zoo?"

She shook her head. "Is that so unbelievable?" she asked, tilting her head and trying to smile, maybe in a flirty way, but she wasn't any good at flirting. At least she never tried to anyway.

"It's not. And that's fine. Actually, that's pretty neat. I get to be with you on your first petting zoo visit." He said it like it was a big deal.

"Sure. You can teach me all the petting zoo etiquette and give me insider tips."

They strolled along, enjoying the ducks and geese, which Mav warned her liked to chase people, so he goofed off by putting her in front of him like a human shield as they walked by.

She laughed and reminded him that he was supposed to be the head of their home, which included protecting people from geese.

He replied that the next time he would bring a shotgun, and *then* he would go first.

After they were through, he pretended to be astounded at her bravery, walking by geese without even carrying a gun.

She rolled her eyes and realized by the time they were done walking the trail and arrived back at the lawyer's office door that she had laughed more in that hour and a half than she had laughed in a long time.

Being with Mav probably had that effect on a lot of people.

Almost disappointed when it was time to open the door, she laughed at herself again, and while he still had his hand on the knob, before he opened it, she looked at him and said, "Is it terrible that I'm disappointed that we're going to go and talk about one billion dollars? That's not normal, is it?"

"I think it means that you've had so much fun, you're loath to see it end. And I have to admit, I am too." This time when he opened the door, he put a hand on her shoulder and guided her through.

He kept it there as the door swung shut behind them, and they stood on the opposite side of the little hut, facing the little man with the spectacles.

He was perusing a large and dusty book and looked up with surprise as they walked in. As though he wasn't expecting them.

"Good afternoon, I'm Peregrine Czeitzler, Esq. Is there something I can help you with?" he asked, like they hadn't just bought petting zoo tickets from him an hour and half ago and told him that they wanted to talk to him about some business.

"You sure can. We have a letter stating that if we got married, we would inherit one billion dollars. I've been trying to call, and I haven't been able to get anyone on the phone."

"Oh, that's too bad. My phone service has been spotty lately. I really need to upgrade, but I just haven't wanted to part with my old phone." He nodded to the side, and Cassie followed his gaze to a rotary phone that had a cradle on the top. The kind that a person saw in a museum and not a lawyer's office.

No wonder the phone wasn't working. She didn't say that, and Mav seemed to restrain himself as well.

"It's a good thing I didn't think to keep trying. I'm pretty sure I would never have gotten a hold of you that way."

"Oh, she's been dependable now for the last fifty years, and my father used her for seventy years before that. I just hate to give her up."

"Yeah. I guess sometimes you get attached to things." As Mav said that, his hand tightened around her shoulder, pulling her even closer. She wasn't sure whether that was on purpose or an accident, but he gave her the feeling that she was something that he was getting attached to. She liked that.

Even as she remembered in the letter that it said that they had to stay married or they had to give the money back.

But she didn't really think that that was why he was attached to her. Would he really pretend to laugh with her and have a good time if he was only thinking about the money?

Of course, he'd asked her about the money this morning at breakfast. It did seem to be something that was on his mind, while she seemed to keep forgetting about it.

She supposed it didn't really matter, but her woman's heart wanted to be wanted for herself, and for whatever he saw in her that he loved, and not because she represented keeping or losing one billion dollars. Even though that was a lot of money.

"The letter's legit, if that's what you're here to ask. That seems to be the main question of people who get the letter."

"Is this a common thing that I've never heard of?" Mav asked.

"Not really. But there have been multiple people who have gotten it. All living in the state of North Dakota, of course. You are just one of many."

"All right. I just got married yesterday. But we forgot to get a license, and so the preacher married us, but we didn't actually have the license until today. Is that going to be a problem?"

"Did the preacher marry you today too?"

"He had a short ceremony, because he said he didn't want to lie on whatever forms he had to fill out. But we had the full vows yesterday."

"I see," the man said, sounding like he was thinking and very unsure. "I'm sorry. I don't know the answer to this question. I will have to do some research, talk to the philanthropist who is giving out the money, and I'll have to get back to you." He gave his phone a baleful glance. "Probably after I get a new phone system installed. It could be several weeks. Maybe a month. I have to make the phone call, then I suppose... Do you mind if I borrow your phone?"

Mav blinked, and it was all Cassie could do not to laugh. The lawyer was asking to borrow their phone?

She tried hard not to giggle as Mav said, "Sure," and he pulled his phone out of his pocket.

He unlocked it with his password before handing it over.

"What did you just punch in?" the little man asked.

"My passcode. The phone is locked without it."

"Interesting. With my phone, I just pick it up and start dialing."

"Yeah. Things have changed a little since Bessie was a baby."

Cassie wanted to laugh so bad, but she managed to just shake her shoulders a bit and keep her lips tightly closed.

Mav's hand squeezed her arm, as though he were noticing that she was trying not to laugh. She definitely couldn't look at him, or she would giggle, and that would be terrible. She wouldn't want to insult the man. He'd been so kind, even if he was a little eccentric.

They waited while he made a phone call, using an actual phone book to find the phone number he was looking for. That place sent him to someone else, and he ended up making four calls before he was able to talk to the person he needed. At least lawyers went through the same troubles that they did when they needed to get in touch with the telephone company.

It was a half an hour or more before they were on their way, with Mr. Czeitzler promising he would call them when he found out for sure what was going on with their money.

"We probably should have just asked him to call his philanthropist from your phone while he was holding it and calling everyone else in the state," Cassie said as they pulled out on the highway.

"Hey, that is a good idea. I never even thought about that." Mav laughed, shaking his head.

"Are you disappointed?" she asked, feeling that he must be but noticing that he didn't seem like he was.

"I'm not. It'll either work out or it won't. I guess... I guess when I was standing in front of the entire town and didn't know if anyone was stepping up, I had resigned myself to the idea that I might lose the farm. Right now, with you beside me, I don't want to, because I need to provide for you, and some of the things I was thinking I might do are things that I wouldn't consider as a married man, because I'd have to leave you alone for a long time. But interestingly, having you beside me makes me feel protective and responsible, but it also gives me...a feeling of lightness I didn't have before."

She wasn't expecting him to say anything like that, and she definitely wasn't expecting the way it made her heart trip and her stomach curl.

"Really?" she couldn't stop herself from saying.

"Is that so crazy? It definitely isn't something I was expecting, but it's true. I've had more fun with you today than I've had with anyone in a long time. And we've just been running errands. We've not been doing anything that's supposed to be fun. I guess what they say about how much fun you have just depends on who you're with is true."

"It always has been for me. Being with you makes everything more fun."

"Maybe that'll wear off." He lifted a shoulder. "I think it probably depends on whether we allow it to or not. You know?"

She nodded, knowing exactly what he was saying. A lot of times, people stopped caring about their marriage, or caring about laughing and having a good time with their spouse, or thinking about how much they enjoyed spending time with them. It just became the same old same old.

"We're always looking for that new high. The new people, we run after them, trying to make them like us. And..." He eyed her. "I'm terrible at that. And I know I am. I know I'm the kind of person who likes to meet new people, and I've done that to my family more than once, I've kind of ditched them for my new friends at times. And often, my new 'friends' aren't people who stand by me. I'd be better off nurturing the...relationships," he grinned at her, "that I have than trying to find a bunch of new ones."

"That's wise," she said simply, knowing it to be true. She thought that maybe their relationship had a chance after all.

Chapter 16

June sat on the edge of her hospital bed, tired, hurting, and discouraged.

"I'm sorry. If you can't get your husband to pick you up today, the doctor is not going to release you."

"All right," June said. "What if I have a friend come?"

"I'll talk to him, but he always prefers to have someone who lives in the house with you pick you up. If your husband can't do it, and you don't have anyone else who is living with you, he thinks it would be better for you to stay in the hospital, where someone is going to be caring for you."

June swallowed her disappointment and nodded, watching as the nurse carried her tablet against her chest while she walked away, nodding at the other person in the room as she walked out.

Her roommate was watching TV, and the sound drifted over toward her. Used to a quiet house, it had bothered her last night when she'd been trying to sleep.

She would sleep better at home, but maybe it was best if there was someone watching and taking care of her, because Wayne almost certainly wasn't going to be.

He stayed for her surgery, but once they put her in a room, he spent two hours on his phone before he said that he needed to go and take care of business.

She'd been surprised that he managed to stay that long.

Maybe when she was younger, a young girl, full of hopes and dreams, she would have been hurt when he didn't stay, but now it's just what she expected.

Part of her wondered if she was settling, but another part of her said that she didn't have a biblical reason to divorce her husband, so she had no choice but to accept the way he treated her and choose to love him and be happy anyway.

She'd tried, multiple times before, to talk to him. To ask him to be more attentive, to care about her. But how did you ask someone to care about you? How did you demand that?

Especially since he knew she didn't believe in divorce, he could treat her however he wanted to. And he did.

God sees. God sees everything. He's not going to let this go unaccounted for. You'll be rewarded for your love and for your kindness. For your actions. And so will Wayne.

The voice was there, every time she wondered if she was making the right decision. Letting her know that God hated divorce. He hated it. He hated when people made a vow and didn't keep it. He hated that something that had been joined together as one was split into two.

She wasn't going to be the one to do it. And Wayne seemed content with the status quo.

She had only texted him before. Deciding that she'd call him to see if he would come, she gingerly reached over to the rolling stand where her phone sat, along with the remnants of her breakfast tray.

She did feel wobbly, and she appreciated the doctor looking out for her. Even if she wished it was her husband who cared.

But she'd sleep better if she was home than in the hospital, and she'd be more comfortable at home.

She wouldn't allow her eyes to water. It wasn't a big deal. She just wanted to go home.

Pulling up his contact, she put the phone to her ear.

She almost thought he wasn't going to answer, but then on the sixth ring, just before it went to voicemail, she heard his voice.

"Hello?"

"Wayne. Did you get my text?"

"The one that said you were able to go home? I answered."

"I know. I was asking about the one that said that the doctor wouldn't let me go home unless the person who was staying with me came and got me. He does not want me there by myself."

"You might be better off in the hospital. It will be late when I get home tonight, and I'm not going to be there. If you need care, the hospital's the best place for you to be."

She wished she could turn those words into something that symbolized care, but she'd been married to him long enough to know that he was basically saying he was busy, didn't want to take the time to go pick her up, and definitely didn't want to have to take care of her after he brought her home.

"Could you take off work this afternoon and tomorrow?"

"I'm really busy. I wish I could. Just stay in the hospital as long as they'll let you, and work on getting better."

She ground her teeth together and counted to five before she said, "All right. Thank you."

"Did you nccd anything else?"

She almost laughed. What was he going to do, bring it to her? If he wouldn't come and pick her up, what did it matter to him if she needed anything?

"I'll call you if I think of anything," she said, her voice cracking a little with the tears she refused to allow to fall, and then hung up the phone.

She sat on the bed trying to hold her tears back, trying not to be discouraged and allow the brain to go to the place it always wanted to.

Why doesn't he love me? Why doesn't he care? Why does he always think whatever he is doing is so much more important than me?

She'd be willing to bet he was probably doing something for the neighbor. They had a new neighbor who just moved in, and Wayne loved new people, new attention, new people to impress. People who didn't know that he never kept his word, didn't do what he said he was going to do, and never paid for anything.

He was charming, and people liked him right off the bat. They didn't see the shady underside of him until they'd been around for a while. Until the glow of them being new had worn off, and he started treating them the way he treated her. Which was like she was disposable.

Of course, he cared for her in his own way, and she figured he would probably be pretty upset if she left. After all, every time one of his relationships blew up with one of the new people that he'd attached himself to, he came back and spent time with her, being nice, like he was soothing himself by spending time with someone he knew loved him.

She knew he loved her. It wasn't true love, it was just the kind of love where he wanted her when he needed her, and when he didn't, he wanted her to be self-sufficient and not bothering him.

Several hours later, June sat in her bed with the covers pulled up, resigned to the idea that she was probably going to be spending another night in the hospital, and slightly dozing, tired and sore, still sleepy from the effects of the anesthesia and the pain medicine that she was taking.

"June," a voice said, and she opened her eyes.

It was the nurse from earlier.

"My shift is almost over, and I'm just checking on you before I leave. I did talk to the doctor, and he said that if you had someone who would come get you and stay overnight with you, you can go home."

"All right. Thank you. Would you get the paperwork started so I can be discharged?"

"You have someone?"

"I do," she said with confidence, knowing that any one of her friends would come and do that for her. They'd even take her to their house. She wanted to go home, but she'd settle for just getting out of the hospital.

"All right. Can I get you anything else before I go?" the nurse asked with a friendly smile.

"No thank you," June said simply, relieved that she wasn't going to be stuck here another day.

Feeling very unloved.

The nurse seemed to pity her, because she knew she had a husband, and she also knew that her husband hadn't been in since yesterday morning. June wondered how many other women sat in the hospital alone, as their husbands did whatever it was that they felt like doing, while they recovered from serious cancer surgery. The doctor had already told her it would be next week before they got the results of the extra tissue that they had taken back, so they could know for sure they had gotten all the cancer.

Right now, she was drowsy, she hurt, and she didn't really care. Now that her youngest child had gone to college, would it matter if she died?

Her husband would just find someone else to take advantage of. When she was younger, she dreamed of having a lifetime love. Someone who admired her, respected her, thought she was amazing. Someone she admired and respected and loved in return. She wanted to feel cherished. To have a friendship, where she laughed and enjoyed someone's company and had someone who laughed at her jokes and she enjoyed theirs.

Wayne acted like she was the stupidest person alive if she made a joke, if he was even around to hear, since usually he wasn't.

He usually wasn't unkind to her, exactly, although everything in the house had to be done his way. The heat was set to where he wanted it, they ate what he liked, they went where he wanted to go and didn't go where he didn't want to go. Life was all about him.

She had been pretty easygoing and typically didn't complain. If ever. She couldn't remember the last time she'd complained.

But there was just a part of her that longed to be loved. To be cherished, the way God made women to be loved and cherished.

It was never going to happen with Wayne.

And she knew it. The temptation to leave her marriage and find someone who would love and cherish her was strong, but that wasn't what the Bible said to do. The Bible didn't promise her a life of being loved and cherished. The Bible commanded her to keep her word. That a vow made to the Lord was sacred. That God hated divorce. And she couldn't vow her life to someone and then walk away just because she wasn't getting what she wanted out of it. As much as she might want to.

Picking up her phone, she called Miss April. Knowing Miss April would come get her. Her husband would probably ride along with her and give her a hand.

As she figured, Miss April answered right away and jumped at the chance to do something for her—even take her home and stay overnight with her.

June told her not to rush, because the paperwork would probably take a while.

She figured that probably fell on deaf ears and Miss April would be in as soon as she could possibly make it.

Telling Miss April that she felt fine, just a little groggy from the medicine, they said goodbye and she let her phone drop in her lap.

Miss April had never told her to divorce her husband, although she knew more about June's marriage than any other person alive did. June didn't complain about her husband to his family, or her family, not to anyone. Although, her kids had moved out as soon as they were able to, to get away from him.

It had broken her heart that they hadn't stuck around, but she understood. If she were free to go, she couldn't say that she wouldn't leave too.

She was just bound by the vows she'd said.

Maybe other women could leave, maybe other women would tell her she should, she just couldn't. She appreciated Miss April not judging her for staying. Like so many women would.

They didn't understand how seriously she took her vows before God.

They didn't understand how clearly she saw that God wanted her to stay and that God would reward her for doing right, and He would eventually judge her husband. She didn't hate her husband and didn't want to see Wayne punished, but God clearly said they would be rewarded according to their works.

For her, that came down to a matter of whether or not she trusted the Lord. If she did, then she would stay. She would believe that God would make things right. She would believe that God would make up for all the nights she lay in bed alone and crying. For all the times she stayed home while he went off with his newest friend, doing things that she had longed to do but that he wouldn't do with her.

She believed God, and so she stayed.

Her phone rang as it sat in her lap, and she swiped to answer, seeing her friend Helen was calling.

"Hello," she said, trying not to sound as groggy as she felt.

"June, sweetie. I wasn't sure if you were out yet or not, and I was going to come visit you if you're still in."

"I'm being released shortly. I'll be home this evening."

"Oh." Miss Helen sounded surprised, then she said, "I saw your husband at the hardware store. He said he was picking up material for Shayna's fence. Apparently, he's helping her fix it today."

She didn't think he was working at his job. Figures. Shayna's fence was more important than picking his wife up at the hospital.

She tried to stop those negative thoughts as soon as they came into her head, but it was hard. And getting harder. Because she suspected that perhaps her husband had not been faithful, although she'd never caught him in infidelity.

Lord? Is it wrong of me to hope that he was? If he was unfaithful—You say divorce is allowed for fornication. Wouldn't that be the one time that I would be allowed to divorce him?

She didn't know what the Lord was thinking, and she was ashamed that the idea of her husband cheating on her didn't cause her sadness. Rather, she felt excitement.

Well, there was sadness, too. Sadness that she hadn't been enough, hadn't been good enough. That her dreams of having a lifelong marriage would be shattered, that the idea of celebrating her golden anniversary, like she had dreamed of on her wedding day, wouldn't come true.

"That must be what he was doing. He didn't tell me. He just said he was working." If her voice sounded sad, she hoped Helen would hear tiredness instead.

But it didn't change the fact that the idea that her husband would rather help the neighbor than come pick her up tore her heart. Not in a way that ripped it apart because she loved him, just in a way that devastated her because he didn't care. And she wanted so badly to have someone, to be married to someone who cared about her and put her first.

Maybe that just wasn't what God had planned for her life.

That was her motto: *Trust God to make things work.*

If they didn't work out this side of heaven, she would trust that they would work out when she got home. To her heavenly home.

With the cancer, it might be sooner rather than later.

Chapter 17

Mav stood with his wife, mingling with the churchgoers as people slowly filed out.

For the first time in his life, he'd sat in church with his arm around a girl, and he had to admit, he had enjoyed the service much more from just that one small change.

He grinned. He probably shouldn't tell the pastor that his sermon was much more interesting when he had a lady snuggled up beside him. But not just any lady. His wife.

Cassie.

It had taken most of the day on Friday to get things straightened out with the lawyer and their marriage license.

On the way home from visiting the lawyer and the petting zoo, they'd stopped to eat.

Yesterday, Cassie had told him she needed to finish a project. It was due Monday, and she didn't want to wait to do it until the last minute.

Last night, she'd gotten it finished, but they hadn't gotten any of her house packed up at all, so that was on the agenda for the coming week.

He'd taken the time yesterday to check his cattle, saddling up his horse by himself and thinking that the next time he did, maybe Cassie would go along. He wanted to ask her whether having cancer would keep her from doing any of the activities that he considered normal, but she seemed a little sensitive on the subject, and he didn't want her to think that it made a difference.

He just wanted to know so that he didn't suggest they do something that she couldn't. Or that she felt compelled to do something that she shouldn't.

He didn't think she would do that. She seemed like the kind of person who wasn't afraid to say no if she needed to, but he didn't want her to be in any danger at all.

Still, this afternoon he had told her that he had promised Jane that he would go to her cooking class in return for her allowing him to sit in her diner all day.

Cassie had laughed and said that probably brought in customers, and he had to laugh with her and admit that she was right.

He liked that she had a sense of humor, and he also really liked that she saw angles that he didn't. Their differences were stark, pretty much in everything they did, but the different ways that they came out in things was very complementary, and he felt like a whole person when he was with Cassie.

Not that he had felt like less than a whole person before Cassie had come along, but just being with her made him realize how much better he could be with someone like her beside him.

He honestly didn't want to go to the cooking class, but he'd promised Jane, and he wanted to keep his word.

He admitted as much to Cassie over breakfast that morning, and she had said the same thing. That he needed to keep his word.

So, he walked her to her house and then kept on walking down to the diner. He saw the little girls had already changed out of their Sunday clothes and were playing outside.

Jane's two children and another little girl he recognized but could not remember her name.

Cassie would be able to remember. Cassie would call her by name and make some comment that would make the little girl feel like Cassie paid attention to her and knew her. The way Cassie did with everyone. Made them feel known and loved like she cared.

And it wasn't just a front she put on. She truly did care. He was seeing that as he spent time with her. Maybe that was one of the ways that having cancer changed her. She saw other people, saw how they really were, saw their aches and pains that other people might overlook, and was able to truly care about them. And let them see that.

It was definitely an area where he could use some work, although the person he most wanted to know that he cared was Cassie.

Hoping that the cooking class didn't take too long, because he wanted to go home and spend time with his wife, he walked in, the bell jingling overhead.

Jane stood in the back, and three older men were already there. Someone had told him in church today that the old men didn't miss a class, although Jane's classes had been a little bit sporadic, and this was the first class they'd had in a while.

He didn't catch the reason, but he figured it wasn't important. As long as they were having class today, he'd show up.

He wasn't going to promise any more classes though, not unless Cassie could come.

He kind of got the feeling that he might be a little bit smitten. After all, she seemed to have turned his insides wrong side out. And bewitched him in that he only wanted to be with her.

Not just because she made him laugh, but there was that.

"Hey, we have a new guy!" Marshall said, jerking his head at Mav as he walked in, like the other guys hadn't already seen him.

"He needs a hairnet," Mr. Blaze said, jerking his own head at Miss Jane, and the five strands of hair he had on his head waved in the breeze just slightly.

"Well," Jane said, a little flustered. "I... I don't have any hairnets," she said all in a rush.

"You don't have to admit that. We'll handle it the way we usually do," Junior said, grinning, maybe because he was the only one of the men who had enough hair to actually need a hairnet.

"Thank you. I know you would, but it always feels awkward. I guess I thought it might be better if I just admit it straight up." She shook her head. "We've been doing this long enough that you'd think I'd remember to order them, but it just keeps slipping my mind. I always have it on something else, and I never think about hairnets. They just don't seem important when I'm thinking about all the other things I want to do."

"It's fine. My hair is pretty short. And I wouldn't want anyone to take a picture of me with a hairnet on. It might go viral."

"You think so," Junior said eagerly, reaching in his back pocket for what Mav could only assume would be his phone.

"No. I was kidding about that. No one wants to see me in a hairnet." Mav spoke hastily, afraid that the old man actually was going to pull his phone out. And while he didn't think anyone would want to see him in a hairnet, there were probably a lot of people who would laugh about it. And he'd prefer not to have his face plastered all over social media looking ridiculous.

That had happened to him enough in his life, and as he got older, he'd gotten less inclined to enjoy it and more inclined to want to keep a low profile.

Junior looked disappointed, and to Mav's relief, he left his phone in his pocket.

"All right, we're going to try something new today. I've been working on this recipe, and I think I pretty much have it, other than maybe just one more thing that I think I need."

"We can help you with that," Mr. Blaze said confidently.

"I was kind of hoping you guys would," Jane said, and Mav couldn't figure out whether she meant that or not.

Jane seemed like the kind of person who was nice to everyone, always with a kind word, and a hard worker too.

Although, after the last few days with Cassie, he was grateful that Jane had seen that they weren't a good fit and had turned him down.

He wouldn't have nearly the fun with Jane that he was having with Cassie. In fact, he almost thought he ought to thank her.

"We're going to use the Instant Pot today. Which is something we haven't used before." She looked around at the three men. "Do you guys have one?"

"No. That's an odd-looking contraption," Marshall said. "Is it dangerous?"

"Not if you use it correctly," Jane said.

That didn't really reassure Mav. Something which had to be used correctly in order to not be dangerous was dangerous to him, since he was very likely going to use it in such a way that it was going to be dangerous.

He didn't say that to Jane now, and none of the other men corrected her either. She talked about butter and then chicken, and then she showed them how to use the various controls on the contraption that she called an Instant Pot.

By the time she was done, she had something that looked pretty good, and she gave them each a spoon, telling them to dip it in, taste it, and see if there was anything that they thought that it needed.

Mav wasn't a big mushroom fan, but he was guessing that Cassie probably loved them, since it seemed that whatever he didn't like, she did. Kind of funny the way they were opposite in pretty much every area. Figuring that there were probably a few things he didn't like that he maybe ought to learn to, he deliberately picked up a mushroom and tasted it.

He was hardly the person to ask if a spice needed to be added, and to him, it tasted pretty much the same way it had when she'd fed it to him on his wedding day. Still, he'd do the best he could.

Indeed, as he tasted it, there was still just a little something missing.

"Think it needs more salt," Marshall said.

"You think everything needs more salt," Blaze said.

"I do not. Potato chips don't need more salt."

"You're not supposed to be eating potato chips anyway," Junior chided him.

"Soy sauce," Mav said. He wasn't sure where that had come from.

Jane's eyes grew big. "That's a really great idea. I never even thought about it. Soy sauce... Yeah."

Mav grinned. He wouldn't have thought about soy sauce, except he and Cassie had made chicken last night after she had gotten done with her project, and it had onions and rice and lots of soy sauce. He hadn't realized that he loved soy sauce, because he never really cooked, until last night.

"You are brilliant," Jane said, getting a measuring spoon and measuring out some soy sauce to add to the chicken, then stirring it.

"I can't take credit for that. I cooked with Cassie last night, and she used soy sauce with the chicken she made, and it was really amazing. I... I guess the idea just came to me after seeing what she did."

"Then I'll have to thank Cassie, because I'm pretty sure that is going to make this dish. I can make it in a bigger quantity now, now that I know the exact recipe. But let's taste it just to be sure."

"Beginner's luck," Marshall mumbled, giving Mav a glare.

Mav just grinned. "Married man's luck," he said, unable to keep the cheesy grin from growing even bigger.

"Rub it in. We're all single. You're just trying to make us feel bad."

"I'm not. Honest. Just happily married." And he realized that was the truth. He really was happily married.

Jane came back with fresh spoons for everyone and asked them to take another taste.

He couldn't believe what a difference a small amount of liquid made, but he had to say, "It's perfect now."

Jane, blinking and holding her spoon, nodded her head. "I have to agree. I wouldn't have thought about it without you, but that's exactly what it needed."

She divided the chicken out for everyone to take home, and Mav packed it up, eager to get back to Cassie.

The men stayed, talking quietly together, like they had something they wanted to do. Mav didn't pay too much attention to them, because Cassie was waiting.

And he wanted to get to her.

Chapter 18

"Did you bring our list?" Merritt asked as the older men filed outside and stood in front of them.

Mr. Marshall nodded. "We made a list. We think you're going to like it."

"All right," Merritt said, looking around at her sister, Sorrell, and their friend Toni.

Usually Sorrell took the lead, but Merritt, who was the youngest of their group at eight, to Sorrell and Toni's nine, decided it was about time for her to take things into her own hands.

She wasn't getting any younger, and she needed a dad.

"Let's see it," Sorrell said, holding her hand out.

"Hang on a second. I need to get my glasses on," Mr. Marshall said while Merritt and Sorrell and Toni waited impatiently.

Merritt tapped her foot, unable to keep herself still.

Maybe when she turned nine, she'd be a little more mature and able to wait without moving like Sorrell and Toni.

"All right," Mr. Marshall said as he held the paper up in front of his nose. "The first one on the list is Paul, from down the street."

"Mr. Paul?" Merritt said, aghast. "But...he doesn't even go to church."

"You didn't tell us that he had to go to church."

"Of course we want him to go to church. How's he supposed to teach us how to be good productive people, if he's not a Christian himself?"

"Just because he doesn't go to church doesn't mean he's not a Christian," Mr. Blaze said, lifting his brows like Merritt was being judgmental.

She didn't want to be judgmental, but she had specific characteristics she wanted in her father, and one of those characteristics was that he had to go to church.

After all, a lot of times she didn't feel like going to church, and if she had a dad who didn't go, she might stop going altogether. And then where would she be?

"How about you just give him a try. Maybe he'll go to church if he gets hooked up with your mom," Junior said.

"No. We need someone who goes to church already. Mom wouldn't even consider someone who's only going because of her. I know that, and we're not going to waste our time. Plus, I don't want someone who goes to church because of me. I want someone who goes to church because of God." Merritt knew she sounded a little bratty, but Paul was not going to cut it.

She hoped Mr. Marshall's list got better, or she was going to be very disappointed.

Sorrell had a great idea, she'd shared it with them just that morning, and she knew it would attract the lady that the men were wanting. But if they didn't give them anything in return, she wasn't sure whether she wanted to share the great idea with them or not.

"Well, I guess we'll have to work on a new list, because none of these men are going to work. I only had two other ones, and neither one of them goes to church, either. I figured you were looking for someone your mom didn't know, and she knows all the men at church."

"I know. We asked you to do something pretty hard," Toni said, sounding mature. She also sounded compassionate, as though she felt bad for the old men and appreciated them trying.

Merritt wanted to stamp her foot. She appreciated them trying, but she wanted them to try harder. Her mom needed a husband, and she needed him now.

"I suppose you don't have to share your information with us, since we let you guys down," Mr. Marshall said slowly, folding the list and shoving it in his pocket.

Merritt had opened her mouth to say, yes, don't bother, but Sorrell uncrossed her arms.

"No. We're going to keep our end of the bargain. You guys tried. We didn't say you had to come up with a list that had someone that would work. We just said you had to come up with a list. You did what you said you were going to do, and so we will too."

Merritt glared at her, but she didn't say anything. If she argued with her sister, she just called her a little girl who didn't understand, and maybe that was true. Because deep down, Merritt knew that she needed to go along with what Sorrell and Toni had already discovered, they had to keep their word, even if they weren't satisfied with what the other person did.

After all, God didn't judge them based on other people. He judged them based on themselves.

She knew that, but she didn't have to like it.

Then, as soon as she thought that, she apologized to the Lord. After all, as her mom had said over and over, "If God could make the world, He could make rules that didn't make sense, even if we don't understand them. He certainly knows how to raise us, and so we need to listen."

"Really? You're still going to help us?" Mr. Blaze asked, sounding like he didn't believe it.

"We will." Sorrell leaned in a little, after looking at both Merritt and Toni, who leaned in with her.

"This is what we think we should do," Sorrell said. "You have your phone. What you need to do is take a video of yourself and post it on your channel. In the video, you're going to say, 'we're three old coots with a cooking show, and we're looking for a lady who will cook for us.'"

"That's it?" Mr. Marshall asked, his brows going down.

"Yep. That's all you have to do. Short videos get lots of views, and you guys will look sufficiently sad, and you'll pull the heartstrings of ladies, and they will flock to come see you." Sorrell sounded confident, and Merritt had to agree.

It was a simple plan, but one that was sure to work.

"Should we take a video now?" Mr. Marshall asked. "I can hardly videotape us and talk at the same time."

"You actually can, but it probably would be best if I take the video. I know your password, and I can post on your account."

"Should I comb my hair?" Mr. Blaze asked, tenderly touching the five strands that were left on his head.

"I think it looks okay. If you look a little disheveled, you look even more needy."

"Good point," Mr. Blaze said, dropping his hand and standing shoulder to shoulder with Mr. Marshall and Mr. Junior.

"All right. We can take it several times if we need to, but just basically say what I said, which is who you are and what you want. A lady."

"Can we start talking?" Mr. Marshall asked.

"Yes. I'm recording."

"You mean that's going to go on the video?"

"Yes."

Merritt knew there were ways to edit the video, and Sorrell and Toni both knew how, but they might not edit it, just because having the men say that would be funny. And funny videos did really well.

"Hi. I'm Marshall. This is Blaze and Junior, and we're three old coots. We're making a channel, and we need a lady. One who can cook, who is funny, and who doesn't need money. Because we're not making any money right now, but we're going to be rich. We'll share with you when we are." He looked at Sorrell, who clicked off on her phone, then clicked and swiped with her thumbs.

"How did we do?"

"That was perfect. That's the only take we need," Sorrell said, with a sly grin tilting at the corners of her mouth. Toni had that same grin on her face, and Merritt figured they both thought the video was going to accomplish exactly what they wanted it to.

Chapter 19

Monday morning, it wasn't quite as much of a shock to Cassie when she walked into the room to see Mav sitting in a chair, one ankle resting on top of the other knee and his fingers on the table.

They weren't drumming, like they had been before, but even though his pose would seem to be casual, he always had a sort of electric energy about him.

It was magnetic to her, but she didn't understand it, either. Because she didn't have anything of the sort.

If anything, she was rather boring, completely content to sit still, and often had to force herself to move.

Mav seemed to be of the opposite persuasion, where he had to force himself to sit still.

Regardless, she was able to smile and say, "good morning," as she carried Phyllis into the kitchen.

"It's definitely better now that you've walked into the room," he said, and she could feel herself blushing, although she figured it was probably a line he used on everyone.

Somehow, the lines he used on everyone didn't mean as much as the ones she felt were specifically tailored for her.

That just made sense. But she wasn't going to complain. He had taken the pains to say something nice, and she certainly wasn't going to discount that.

Opening the door and setting Phyllis outside, she stood back up and closed it.

"Coffee?" she asked, although she was pretty sure she knew the answer to that.

"Yes please." He paused. "I almost made some, but I wasn't sure what time you were going to get up, and while I can drink cold coffee, I prefer it fresh."

"Me too. And this is pretty much my usual time." It was the same time she'd stepped into the kitchen the last time he'd been there.

"I'm learning that," he said, a little bit of humor in his voice, and she smiled along with him.

"Are we making breakfast together again?" he asked.

She loved that he wasn't acting like he was the boss but that he also wasn't walking around on tenterhooks, afraid to offend her. He just acted like he belonged there, which he did.

She wanted him to. Even though, they'd agreed that they were going to start cleaning her house in preparation for putting it on the market to sell.

It was a big day, and maybe she should have gotten up earlier.

"Sure. We have a lot of work to do, and a big breakfast is essential."

"I agree that food is essential. Sometimes I'm not hungry first thing in the morning. If I get up at four, it's usually about this time when I'm ready to eat."

"This time" was seven o'clock. Four seemed awfully early.

"Were you up at four?" she asked, trying not to sound too surprised. Maybe that's the time ranchers always rose. She wouldn't know.

"I was. I was up at three but lay in bed until four. Guess I was feeling a little lazy this morning."

"So did you go to bed at seven last night?" she asked, knowing that he left her house shortly after supper.

"No. It was more like midnight."

"So you only had three hours of sleep?" She could hardly believe it. That seemed crazy.

Bending over, she got the eggs and bacon out of the refrigerator, as well as some cheese and a few veggies. She liked an omelet better than she liked plain eggs, anything to drown the taste of the eggs, and she figured she might as well find out if he enjoyed it too.

He was already working on the toast when she set the things down on the counter.

"Are any of these things something that you don't want to have in your eggs?" she asked, indicating the vegetables in front of her.

"If you cook it, I'll eat it." He grinned a little. "You definitely eat a lot healthier than I do. I prefer doughnuts by far, bagels if necessary, but always something quick and easy."

"Carbs."

"Quick energy."

"I like that too. And I probably would eat more like that, but..." She had reprimanded him for reminding her about her cancer, and he had been very sensitive about saying anything after that.

She hadn't meant to be so harsh or to change his actions toward her completely, where he felt like he had to tiptoe around the C word when she was near, so she felt it was a little unfair of her to bring it up, when he seemed to be afraid to talk about it. Because of her.

Maybe they should get that straightened out too.

She had to be able to talk to him about anything, and that meant her past, even if it included talking about her cancer.

"Because of my cancer, I try to eat healthy. I know I'm at risk for it coming back or for me developing a new kind. And I don't want to be legalistic about it, to the point where I won't allow anything that's not homegrown, organic, clean, whole food to touch my lips, but I do try to be more careful."

"I see." He looked over at her thoughtfully, like he hadn't considered that at all. And he probably hadn't. He was young, and from what she understood, it often took a while for men especially to realize that they weren't invincible and that death would eventually happen to all of them.

Because of her illness, she had been a lot more aware of her frailty and how close death really was.

"I guess that's something I'm going to have to change," he murmured.

"I don't want you to have to change your eating habits because of me. I can adjust." She said that, although she didn't really want to. The whole reason that she ate the way she did was so that she might come close to having a lifespan as long as a normal person. For her to stop doing that would mean that she'd most likely die much younger.

"I want you to be around as long as possible. So, if that means I have to change the way I eat in order to accommodate the way you do, that's what I want."

She paused while she was slicing mushrooms and just stared at her hands for a moment. Really? Did he mean that? "So you don't really like the things I'm chopping up?"

"I told you. If you put it in front of me, I'll eat it. And your health is important to me. So if we need to eat a certain way in order for you to be healthy, that's what we're going to do."

She had to blink a few times before she could see. She took a breath before she spoke. "I was not expecting that from you. I appreciate that so much. I didn't want you to have to change your life because of me, and maybe it's not even the fact that you're changing your life, but it's the fact that you want me to be healthy. That you care. That means a lot to me."

That was it. The fact that he cared. That he cared and he wasn't just saying that he cared, in fact, he looked a little surprised when she said that meant he cared.

He wasn't giving lip service, he was putting actions on the ground, *showing* her that he cared. Which meant so much more than saying that he did.

His arms fell from his chest, and he closed the gap between them with one step, putting a hand on her shoulder, touching her gently as he slid it down to her elbow and back.

She had to work to contain the shiver that elicited.

"I'm sorry I'm not very good at letting you know I care. I...I'm a little uncomfortable even talking about it. But not just because you're my wife. I have been having fun with you. But even beyond that, I've been watching you. And feeling that you're someone I can admire. Someone I'm...proud...to be married to. Not proud in a bad way, but proud in a way that I know you love God and you're doing your very best to walk with Him. That makes me feel something big and happy in my chest that I can't really explain." He didn't say anything more.

She felt the hair beside her temple move and realized he had pressed his lips, carefully and gently, on the side of her head.

"You're an amazing woman." His voice was low, and this time, she couldn't contain her shiver.

She was on the verge of turning and putting her arms around him when the toaster popped up.

His hand tightened around her shoulder, and she thought he was going to ignore it, then his lips brushed her skin again, so sweet and gentle it almost brought tears to her eyes, and then he straightened.

"I'm going to have the toast done before you have the veggies chopped," he said, casually, like he hadn't just been whispering sweet nothings in her ear and causing her stomach to pool in a muddled heap at her feet.

"Yeah. I guess I should assign you to cut the vegetables first next time." She knew she sounded a little breathless, like she hadn't quite gotten control over her equilibrium, and there was nothing she could do about it.

There had been a reason she had crushed on him now for such a long time. Who would have thought he would have such a huge effect on her? Just holding her arm and whispering in her ear. It wasn't even really a whisper, he was just stating facts as far as he was concerned.

Still, it took her a while to feel like she was back to normal. In the meantime, Mav chattered about what he'd seen in his herd while he was riding that morning, about his plans for the ranch if the billion dollars came through, and about how long he thought they should wait before they'd call the lawyer to see if he'd heard anything. A week? Two?

Thankfully, this conversation didn't require much effort on her part, and she was pretty much back together by the time the omelets were made, and they put the toast and coffee and eggs on the table.

"Making omelets is a lot more involved than just making eggs."

"It is. It takes more time and effort, but I feel like it's worth it, because they're a lot healthier that way. Although eggs themselves are healthy."

"It's kind of a tricky way to hide vegetables in something."

"I kind of feel like it's the other way around, since I don't like eggs. It's a tricky way for me to hide eggs in with my vegetables."

"You don't like eggs? I've never heard of such a thing."

"I know, right? It's not even that I don't like the taste of them, they just make me feel a little bit weird after I eat them. Vegetables negate that feeling."

"Must be all that wholesome goodness. You just can't stand it, and you have to mess it all up with vegetables."

"Right. That's probably it." She rolled her eyes, and he laughed.

She loved the sweet rapport they seemed to have developed, enjoyment with each other's company that just felt natural. Hopefully it wasn't a flash in the pan and once they got used to each other, they would sit and eat their breakfast in silence like so many couples did.

She didn't want that to happen in her marriage. For her to start sitting across the table from a virtual stranger, unable to engage him in conversation or get him to pay any attention to her.

Mav didn't seem like the kind of person who would ever do that. But he did seem like he was always on the go, always had an idea or something he was interested in, a project he was doing or something to funnel his energy toward.

Speaking of, after he'd said a prayer, she took a forkful of her eggs and said, "So we were going to start packing up my house today. Is that still your plan?"

"It is. I figured I would head down to the hardware store, grab some boxes and a few totes for the more delicate things, unless you have some sitting around, and we'll pack the things we want to take to my ranch in totes and maybe put the things that you want to donate to the secondhand store in garbage bags."

"That sounds good to me. I do have a few totes, but it wouldn't hurt to grab a few more."

He smiled, like he enjoyed her praise, and they chatted while they finished their eggs. If that was the way their breakfasts were going to go for the next fifty years, she looked forward to them.

Chapter 20

Mav walked to the hardware store, wanting to whistle.

He wasn't sure what it was about Cassie that made him so happy, but spending time with her had been fun and enjoyable. How had he ever thought she was boring, and why he hadn't ever noticed her?

She was quiet, and she had a self-containment about her that could be a little bit intimidating. She didn't fidget or make unnecessary movements. Which were something that seemed to be hallmarks of him.

Opposites attract, or at least that's what he had been told, and he supposed that was true in Cassie's and his case, although they had so many things in common that there was glue to keep them together, even if their opposite tendencies tended to push them apart at times.

Of course, like charges repelled, while opposite charges attracted, so maybe having things in common wasn't as important as being able to compromise.

He was thinking so hard as he walked down the sidewalk that he almost missed Miss Charlene as she came toward him.

She was barely a yard away from him when he tipped his hat and said, "Good morning, ma'am."

"Mav Stryker. How is married life treating you?"

"I was just thinking it couldn't really get any better. I'm happily surprised."

"Surprised?" she asked, lifting her brows, then putting one hand on her ample hip.

"Yeah. Maybe I shouldn't admit that, but I was just thinking about how Cassie was kind of quiet and I never really noticed her, but she's funny and sweet and we seem to get along really well." Of course, it had only been a few days. Maybe once the newness wore off, they wouldn't get along so well. But he figured that was probably mostly up to Cassie and him. And he knew Cassie was going to work as hard as she could to get along with him. And he would do the same. He had a lot of optimism for the future.

"I have to say, I'm not sure I would have put you two together. I know I was supposed to have a talent for that, but neither one of you were people I would have chosen. But I would say now that I've seen the light, seen you two together a little bit, you make an excellent team. I bet you'll find that you are much more productive and successful with Cassie beside you. She complements you almost perfectly."

"I have to agree with that, Miss Charlene," Mav said, thinking again that she was probably right. That he could do more with Cassie beside him. Of course, it could go both ways, since he was currently going to the hardware store to help her to get things to help her pack her house up, so he thought he was doing an okay job of doing his part.

"I actually have a question for you, and I was on my way to Cassie's house to see if I could catch you so I didn't have to ride out to your ranch."

"Well, you caught me. Ask away."

"I was hoping you and Cassie might ride in the carriage for the fourth of July parade next week. I have your brother, Cord, signed up to drive his carriage with his Percheron team hitched to it in the parade. I wasn't sure exactly what we should do with the carriage. But I thought we would decorate it with Just Married signs, you and Cassie can dress however you want to, and we'll provide some candy for you guys to throw. That could be, maybe not a honeymoon exactly, but a little special treatment for Sweet Water's newest newlyweds."

"Sounds good." He hadn't talked to his brother Cord in a while, since Cord was busy training his Percherons and making his sleighs. His business had been booming for him in the last few years, and his brothers had been after him to hire help. But he and Rosie were content on their farm by themselves. They didn't want to turn their business into an industry but wanted to keep it with a mom-and-pop bent, including their children and doing what they could.

Unfortunately, the demand was so high that that meant they were busy, although it also meant the busyness allowed them to pay for their farm and their horses, so Mav knew it was a balancing act for them.

"Don't you want to talk to your wife first?" Charlene asked, in a low voice that was almost a reprimand.

"Oh. I'm sure she'll be fine with it," he said, unable to think of any reason why she wouldn't be. After all, it was just riding in a carriage. And she wasn't the one who had trouble sitting still. That was him.

"All right. Well, let me know if you change your mind," Charlene said, a note of warning in her voice.

Mav determined that as soon as he got home, he would make sure that he said something to Cassie, just because of the way Miss Charlene was talking. Still, he really couldn't imagine that there'd be any problem with it.

He said good day to Miss Charlene and continued on down the sidewalk, noticing that Sweet Water's pig, Munchy, was wandering across the road at the far end of town.

So far, no vehicles had hit any of the animals crossing the street, neither the pig nor the Highlander, Billy, who often ran around town chasing the pig for some odd reason.

Mav shook his head. He had a hard time believing all the rumors that went around town about those animals, but small towns liked their eccentricities, and he supposed if that was Sweet Water's claim to fame, he would not be the one to question the accuracy of the reports.

It didn't take much time at all to grab the totes, and although they were bulky as he carried them back, the day was beautiful, in the low eighties, and not too hot, so he hadn't broken a sweat by the time he got back to Cassie's house.

She had the dishes done when he walked in and was working on pulling things from the cupboards and putting them on the table.

"You're back already," she said, turning around.

"Looks like you got a lot done since I left. Dishes are done, and if the stuff on the table is any indication, you have at least seventeen cupboards empty."

She laughed and turned back toward the cupboard she was working on. "That is just one cupboard."

"You're kidding."

"No. I'm dead serious. Do you think we need more totes?" she asked as she turned around with another handful of things, setting it all down on the already overstuffed table.

"No, we have boxes, too, for anything that's not breakable, but you have more things on the table than I have in my entire house."

"Really?" Her voice made her disbelief plain.

"Really." He touched a couple of the spices on the table. "I have salt and pepper, hot sauce, and garlic. I think it's garlic. My sister gave to me when she accidentally bought two. I haven't opened it. But anyway, that's all I have."

"You have salt and pepper and an unknown spice in your cupboard?"

"Hot sauce, too."

"Don't you keep that in the refrigerator?"

"That's my spare bottle."

"All right." She put a hand over the bridge of her nose, like she was getting a headache.

Could her cancer be coming back?

He couldn't believe the pang of fear that shot through him. Then he stepped forward, his hand on her shoulder and another one sliding around her cheek to the back of her neck.

"Are you okay?" he asked, his words rushed but soft, and they held all the concern he felt in his whole body.

He thought she heard it, because her brows lifted, and her eyes, holding surprise, flew to his. "Yes. Fine."

He searched her face, wanting those words to be true but not entirely sure. "You'd tell me if there was anything wrong?"

"You're my husband. Yes. I will tell you."

"That's a promise?"

"Yes. It's a promise." She lifted her shoulder. "Although, if I say it, I hope you can believe that it's true. You don't need to make me promise."

"I think that'll come in time."

It was his experience that sometimes people said things that they didn't really mean. They were just words that came out of their mouth, words they had no intention of following through. He didn't think Cassie was like that, but he supposed after dealing with her for a while, he would know for sure, and then he would know that if she said it, it was true. She would do it.

He didn't like that idea, but he supposed she felt the same way about him, even if he wished she would just believe him now without him having to prove anything.

Just because they had said vows together didn't make them automatically trust each other. Sometimes trust had to be earned.

Although, he should be able to give it to his wife.

"I'm sorry. If you say it, I'm going to assume it's true." If it turned out that that was a bad decision, he'd have to figure out what to do, but it wouldn't be a hardship to just simply believe his wife.

"Thank you," she said, and maybe it was his imagination, but she seemed to push her head into his hand just a little, like she was craving his touch.

But that couldn't be. She had wanted time. And the longer he thought about it, the more he thought that maybe she wouldn't even decide that she wanted to be with him. Not that way. He understood that women were different, and maybe she'd never think of him like that.

He didn't know what he was going to do about that either. There were so many things he didn't know, and he preferred to focus on the things that he did.

He dropped his hand and stepped back, wanting to brush his hands together, like a job was done. But he didn't want her to know how relieved he was that she was okay.

So instead he said, "I saw Miss Charlene in town. She wanted to know if we would ride in a horse-drawn carriage in the parade. My brother Cord driving. I told her it would be no problem."

"What?" Cassie said, freezing with one tote in her hand, a lid in the other. She jerked her head up at him, her eyes wide.

She must have heard him wrong. He couldn't imagine what she thought he said, so he just repeated, "Miss Charlene wanted us to ride a horse-drawn carriage in the parade. My brother Cord will be driving. I told her it'd be fine. I think they're going to put Just Married on the side, and we can dress up if we want to. Since we kind of had a casual wedding."

"She wants us to ride in the parade?"

"Yep."

"In front of all those people? People who will be staring at us as we ride down the street?"

Her tone indicated that maybe it wasn't a matter of simple misunderstanding. That she was really upset. He hated that, because it meant Miss Charlene was most likely right, since she had warned him that he ought to run it over with his wife before he said yes.

He didn't want to have to go back to her and tell her that she had been right and that Cassie didn't want to, but he would. Except, he couldn't understand what the issue was.

"I'm sorry. It's perfectly safe. You know Cord's Percherons are gentle as lambs. I mean, a child could drive them."

"I know. I'm not afraid of the horses."

"I'm not sure what the issue is?"

She took a deep breath, almost as though she were striving for patience or something.

Then, almost as though she'd remembered something, she looked down and blew the breath out, and she seemed like she was warring with herself.

"You told Miss Charlene we'd do it?"

"Yeah. I didn't think there'd be a problem. But if there is, I guess I can tell her it won't work out after all. I feel kinda bad, because I did say yes, but I don't want to force you to do something you don't want to do—?"

He kind of allowed that question to trail off, indicating he was hoping she would tell him what the issue was.

Honestly, he had no idea.

"I'm sorry. I told myself that I would start saying yes, because my automatic answer is often no. And each time God has tested me on it, my automatic answer has been no."

"I see. I guess I have the opposite problem. My automatic answer is sure, why not? And I have a tendency to get myself into things that maybe I shouldn't. It appears I've done it this time too."

"No. You haven't." She put a hand up, stopping him from saying anything more. "I think it's a cute idea. And while I don't have a wedding dress, I definitely could dress up, if you don't mind?"

"I can find a monkey suit to put on, I suppose. Or I could just wear a pair of nice jeans and a button-down. I'd be just as happy in them."

"I think I would be just as happy seeing you in that. Although, I think you'd be dashing in a suit as well."

"And I'd be uncomfortable as—something."

She laughed, and he appreciated the fact that she didn't get upset.

"But I'd do it for you," he added, not really to get on her good side, but he loved the soft look that came into her eyes when he said things that made her feel good. He supposed that was building a relationship like she wanted, and he found that the look in her eyes was reward enough for the things that he tried to do that would build a relationship between them.

"And I appreciate that. But let's not. Let's just do jeans and a button-down, and maybe I can find a skirt and a little bit of a fancy blouse, and you can wear your hat. I don't have one."

"Maybe I can find you one. I could borrow one from my sisters. If you really want?"

"I wouldn't want to put them out."

"Oh, you wouldn't be putting them out. They share clothes all the time. Plus, you need to get integrated into the family anyway. I don't know why I haven't thought about that."

"Maybe because we've been busy doing other things?"

"That's probably why my mom's been texting. I checked it out, and it didn't seem like an emergency, and I kind of forgot about it. She's probably going to want us to go eat with the family. Is that going to be a problem with you?"

"Yes. I mean, no. I would love to eat with the family."

It made him laugh. She was trying. And to see her try made him want to try too. They could figure this out and make it work. No problem.

"You know, I'll just go ahead and tell Miss Charlene that we're not going to do it. It sounded to me like it wasn't the horses that was a problem, but something else?"

"I just… It feels weird to be sitting there in front of people and having them all stare at you. I… I don't like to be the center of attention. I like to be the person behind the scenes being useful. Doing something that contributes but that doesn't draw attention to myself. I feel weird when people are looking at me."

"That's funny. I'm the exact opposite. I love the attention. I thought it was awesome to sit in the carriage, and the only thing that could be better would be to drive it."

"Nobody notices the driver. Everyone's always looking to see who's inside."

"So maybe you should drive the carriage."

She laughed.

"No. I'm serious. Cord's Percherons are really gentle. I wasn't joking about that. And he'll have his gentlest pair to put in the parade. He will not want them to spook or cause any problems. Of course, they're gonna look good too, because he'll have them all dolled up, but you could drive them. It would be fun. I'll sit in the back and wave to people. They can keep the Just Married signs on the side, and we can just be Sweet Water's most eccentric newlywed couple."

She had a smile on her face, and she looked like she was about to laugh, but she still seemed like she wanted to say no, when she had sworn that she was going to say yes. He figured a little prompting wouldn't hurt.

"What about that vow you vowed to yourself? Something about saying yes to opportunities or something?"

"Oh, you're terrible. I can't believe you're throwing that in my face."

"Hey, I think you'll thank me."

"Do you think Cord would mind if I practice first?"

"I know he won't. In fact, he'd probably love it if we'd take his horses out for a ride. They have so many that it takes forever for him to exercise them all, and while he doesn't want to hire help, he doesn't mind family coming in and giving them a hand once in a while. I'll talk to him."

"All right. And you'll promise that if something happens, you won't hesitate to jump in and help me?"

"I won't. But I know you can do it."

Chapter 21

Cassie pulled more Tupperware containers out of the cupboard and set them on the table.

Mav worked silently beside her. They pretty much had the entire kitchen done. She was working on the last cupboard, and he was putting things into boxes.

He seemed antsy though. Like he could barely contain himself in the house.

He was used to being outside. Not stuck indoors. Was that the problem?

Of course, it wouldn't hurt him to learn to do some things that made him uncomfortable. After all, twice this morning she forced herself to say yes when her automatic and preferred answer was no. And of course, she didn't think that she always had to say yes, but she had determined that she said no so many times and to so many things, and that was her default answer, when if she would just think about it, it wouldn't hurt to say yes.

It seemed like Mav thought, why not? That needed to be the way she thought too. Seriously thinking, why not? Because if there was a reason to not, then no was the correct answer.

But if there was no reason to say no, then it shouldn't be the first thing that came out of her mouth.

Riding in the carriage. No, *driving* the carriage?

What were you thinking?

She dreaded it a little bit, but she was also excited. Because it was a new experience. Something that could end up being fun.

She needed to not dread those kinds of things, the crowds and the people staring at her and being the center of attention, and just learn to roll with it.

Mav was really going to be a good teacher in that regard for her.

She glanced over at him, and while there was no outward manifestation of the electricity she felt, she still had the idea that he was feeling stifled.

Maybe she was going to be a good teacher in helping Mav learn how to be bored and content with that.

She didn't really like that thought, and so she set one more group of plastic containers on the kitchen counter, but instead of turning back to the cupboard, she turned to Mav.

"I feel like you could use a break."

His head swiveled to hers, like he hadn't been expecting her to say anything.

They had chatted easily for a while and then fell into a companionable silence, and she was breaking it.

But maybe it was her words, the idea that he needed a break. Since he'd been working for less than two hours.

"I wouldn't take a break without you. Are you getting tired?" His face creased with concern, and he took one step toward her, like he was going to touch her again.

On the one hand, she loved the concern and that he cared about her.

On the other hand, she didn't want to be babied.

She wasn't sure which one was the most dominant, and it didn't matter anyway. Whatever he did, she would appreciate it. If he was caring for her because he was concerned about her cancer coming back, she would appreciate it. And if he was not paying attention and doing things his own way, she would appreciate that too.

She needed to learn to be content with whatever happened.

This whole marriage thing was going to be a good lesson in that. Getting her way sometimes, but not getting her way others, and learning to be content in the fact that she got her way sometimes, so it was only fair that Mav got his way sometimes too.

And she couldn't keep score.

She knew that intrinsically.

"I wasn't thinking that you would take a break from working completely, I was thinking that you'd take a break from being in the house and maybe carry these things that we have to the car? Or your pickup, if that's what you're using? And maybe you can take a load to the drop-off center for the secondhand store?"

One had recently opened in Sweet Water, although she hadn't met the proprietress yet. She hadn't had any reason to go down, because she hadn't needed to buy anything.

Although, curiosity almost overrode her practicality.

"You think that would be a help?" he asked, and while he didn't exactly jump on it, she felt like he was eager to move. To get out. To do something besides stand.

She wasn't sure exactly what, but it wouldn't hurt for him to take some things and deliver them, and maybe that would help whatever she was sensing.

"Yeah. I... I feel like maybe you're ready to go out and move around."

He laughed. "Is it that obvious? I thought I was hiding it. I'm just not used to staying inside."

"No. It really wasn't that obvious. It was just something I... I felt."

She didn't really want to talk about that anymore. Sometimes she could tell what people were thinking, not even by looking at their face but just by their movements and how the air around them felt. Without touching them. She knew that was weird.

She couldn't do it all the time, and she couldn't do it with everyone, but once in a while, she was right.

"I guess we do probably have a load here."

"Yeah. Especially if you take the blankets that I washed and bagged in there in the laundry. I think there's four or five bags. I don't even know where I got so many blankets, but I assume you have some at your house."

"I do," he said, but he didn't sound completely sure of it.

"You have blankets on your bed?" she asked, just to clarify.

"Yeah."

"Do you have blankets on the spare bed?"

"I do. Some. I think."

She laughed.

He held his hands up. "Okay. I'm sorry. I never really paid attention. One of my sisters insisted that I needed a bed for the spare bedroom, so I bought one from an estate sale in Rockerton when I was down there looking at horses. I set it up, and I don't think I've looked at it since. I'm pretty sure it came with blankets."

"We have the blankets that are on my bed. So, as long as your bed has blankets, we don't need any of the extra ones I have. I have one small basket set aside with blankets for the couch—" She had a terrible feeling. "You do have a couch, right?"

"Of course. Actually, I have a recliner. That counts, right?"

"So we should save my couch?"

"Maybe I ought to take you out to my place, you can look around and see what I have, and then decide what we need to keep here."

"That's a really good idea. I should have thought of that myself."

He grinned. "Maybe I'm coming in handy after all?"

"I don't think there was ever any question about whether or not you were going to come in handy."

"Really? Because I got to thinking about us, and you didn't need me at all. You're doing just fine by yourself all this time. I'm the one who was in financial difficulties. I'm the one who had the letter and needed to get married. You didn't. So, I'm not sure what I'm bringing to this marriage, but you didn't need it. Maybe I feel like I need to step up my game a little bit."

"I don't think there's ever any problem if someone wants to step up their game. As long as that means you become a better person."

"Yeah."

"So, keep stepping up. That's fine. I suppose, you inspire me to step up too. Because it's kind of hard to be around someone who is working to be better and not want to be better yourself."

"I know exactly what you're talking about."

They smiled at each other, and she wasn't sure exactly what they'd figured out, but she felt like it was something important. Something important for their relationship. And she liked it.

"All right. Let's load this stuff up in the truck, and then we'll both take a break, take the stuff to the secondhand store, and run out to my place. While I unload it, you can take a look around and see what you think. Sound good?"

"That sounds perfect. I'm totally down for that."

He grinned and went to put his boots on while she finished pulling the plasticware out of the cupboard and packing it up.

She had been worried that there might not be room in his house for all of her stuff, but after what he had been saying, she thought that maybe there was plenty of room, and she was worrying unnecessarily.

He carried things out, and she finished up the packing. She actually packed a couple of boxes of books that she wanted to go to his place, and he was able to carry those out as well, making the pickup rather full.

It wouldn't be quite that much once they stopped at the secondhand store and got rid of all the extra stuff she didn't need.

Maybe she was giving away too much, but a lot of the stuff was stuff that she had gathered over the years and didn't really need. Wasn't that true about almost everything? She didn't really need it, she just liked having her stuff around. Figuring she'd think about that later, she gave Phyllis a pat and followed Mav out the door with each of them carrying a last box.

They rode to the secondhand store, which was closed on Mondays, but the new collection container was open, and they managed to fit all their things in.

They were on the way out to Mav's farm, which she had never seen, when he said, "Do you mind if I call my brother and ask him if it's okay if we come around and practice driving? Not today, but maybe Wednesday? Do you think we'll be done by then?"

"Yeah. That sounds good. As long as I don't get any work between now and then, it should be fine."

She'd never in her life before tried not to get work. She'd always taken as much as she could, just because she never knew when she wouldn't have any or when she might get sick again.

"Hello?"

"Cord, it's Mav."

He put the phone on speaker so he could drive hands-free. Or maybe so she could listen too. She liked to think it was a little of both.

"What's up, little bro?"

"I have a couple questions for you."

"Shoot."

"First of all, you're driving a carriage in the parade next week?"

"Yeah. Miss Charlene asked me to. Why?"

"She asked us, Cassie and me, to ride in the carriage as newlyweds."

"Oh. That's right. Congratulations. Rosie and I have been meaning to stop around. Rosie more than me, but we just haven't had time."

"No, that's fine. It's only been a couple of days, and it was rather unexpected."

"I'll say. And Rosie wants to know all about it, so I hope Cassie is going to be ready for twenty questions when we do meet up."

"Cassie is ready for anything." Mav looked across the seat and winked at her.

She could feel her cheeks heating, but she returned his smile.

"Anyway, Cassie doesn't really want to have a lot of eyes on her, and no one ever looks at the driver, so I suggested she drive. She's...game for the idea, although not particularly eager. Even though I told her that your horses were as gentle as kittens."

"I don't know whether I would go that far. But they're pretty calm. And I know she'd be okay. A child could drive them."

"That's exactly what I told her."

"I guess we agree on something then," Cord said, and it wasn't hard to hear the smile in his voice, like he and Mav hadn't always seen eye to eye.

Mav chuckled, as though he agreed with that. "Anyway, she's never driven before, and I told her that you're always looking for people to come out and exercise your horses for you, and that you probably wouldn't have a problem if we came out to do that and if she practiced with the team you're planning on using in the parade. If that's a problem, we're good with whatever you decide."

"No problem at all. You know you're always welcome here. You know we're always looking for help and love it when it comes from family. And if Cassie is hitched up with you, I'm not sure about her intelligence level, but she's still family."

"I have it on speaker, and she's listening," Mav said, looking across the seat and winking at her again.

She didn't say anything though. She knew Cord from seeing him at church but had never really talked to him. And it didn't seem appropriate for her to butt into the brothers' conversation.

"Hey, Cassie. Sorry about the insult, but I mean, you did marry Mav."

"No problem. You're family, so you can get away with it," she said, imitating what he had said. "Plus, I think maybe there's more to Mav than what you think. You're remembering a little boy, and he's grown up and matured a lot."

Chapter 22

Cassie didn't want to gush on about Mav too much, although maybe she should. Maybe Mav needed people to talk about him and for her to tell other people how wonderful he was, because everyone seemed to have the stigma in their head that he was just like the way he was when he was eighteen. That was ten years ago, and he had grown up.

Even though she loved him then, maybe she loved him in a little girl way, just admiring the energy and the spirit and the sense of humor that he had. But as he matured into a man, she found even more to admire.

"Well, I guess I can say that one smart thing he did was to marry you. I heard good things about you, and I'm glad that my brother found such a wonderful woman to be his wife. I know Rosie can't wait to get together with you and talk."

"And I can't wait to go talk to her. And hang out with the rest of Mav's family," Cassie said, and it was only just a little bit not true.

Large crowds of people sometimes made her nervous, and Mav had a lot of brothers and sisters.

And they had kids, and they were almost to the point where the kids were having kids, and it was going to be loud and crazy if the whole family got together.

That was a far cry from her, who just had her mom and her. Her mom had gotten remarried to a man who didn't have any children, and they were living in California, doing whatever it was that retired couples did when they had a lot of money and a lot of time and no responsibilities.

"All right, Cord, would Wednesday work for you?"

"Sure would. If you text me half an hour before you get here, I'll try to make sure your team's hitched up for you. If not, I'll show you how to do it."

"All right. I'll talk to Cassie and see what she wants, and we'll see you on Wednesday."

"Sounds good."

They hung up, with Mav smiling as he swiped his phone off.

"Sound good to you?" he asked, looking across the seat at her again.

"It does. Thank you. I… I think this is going to be fun."

"I don't know. I think I'd rather have you sit beside me in the carriage, but I think I'll enjoy watching you drive the horses too. So, it's kind of a win-win for me."

"I suppose I would rather be sitting beside you too. But I'm looking forward to driving the horses, so it's a win-win for me too."

He grinned as he put his turn signal on and pointed to the road ahead. "This is my road. My driveway comes off this road in about a mile. So we're almost there."

"You don't live quite as far out as what I thought."

"No. It's just a ten- or fifteen-minute drive into town. More, if it's snowing, of course. Although, I try to hunker down and not do too much in the winter other than check the stock and make sure they're okay. So, even though it's not too far into town, I don't make the trip too much in winter."

"That makes sense."

She watched as they turned in, eager to see where he lived and the ranch he worked.

As they turned on the lane, she said, "Are you going to tell me where your land begins?"

"Sure. You'll see it. I actually have an arch, and we'll drive under it. I didn't make it, the guy who owned the ranch before me did. I have about five hundred acres. I own both sides of the driveway from there to the house, and the house kind of sits in the middle of it. It's actually a pretty nice setup."

"Sounds good. I always loved those old arches. Not too many people do that anymore."

"Pretty expensive, from what I've heard. But since I didn't have to do it, I don't know. Nice to reap the benefits of some other people's work, although I love doing the work myself and reaping those benefits as well."

It was easy to tell when they went under the arch, and she looked around, eager to see when the house came into view.

A pole building that served as his barn with some fencing around it, probably corrals and paddocks that he used to work his cattle, along with a head chute system, came into view first. And then the house. It wasn't anything to speak of, a small ranch-style one that was maybe two or three bedrooms, and a light blue color, which she loved.

It was perfect. Not too big, not too small, and it looked well maintained.

"I don't have any flowers or anything planted. Guess I'm kind of wishing I did right now, because I figured you'd appreciate them. But I just never took time."

"That's okay. That'll give me something to do. I love working with flowers, and that was one of the things I was going to miss at my house, the back porch where I had been setting plants out and having a few small raised bed container gardens in my backyard. I'll eagerly get to work doing some of those things around here."

"I'll help you, if you let me know what you want. If you're looking for raised beds or anything. I can slap some boards together, although I'm not a great carpenter."

"That would be wonderful. I ordered the ones I got, because I'm not a great carpenter either. Actually, I'm not a carpenter at all."

He laughed. "But I bet you put the ones you ordered together yourself."

"I did. And I enjoyed it. It was busywork. Once I figured it out, it was easy, and I could just enjoy the weather and the sounds of nature while I worked."

"That's a lot of what ranching is. It's not hard work, necessarily, it's just everyday work, and a lot of it doesn't take a whole lot of brainpower, so you're free to think or, like you said, to enjoy nature around you."

He sounded a little amazed, like maybe they might have something in common after all, and she didn't want to disabuse him of that notion. Although, she figured that her idea of enjoying the weather for a five-minute break while she walked outside for a few minutes was different than his idea of enjoying the weather for twelve or fourteen hours a day while he was outside in it.

Still, it was a bit of a start.

He pulled up to the house and turned the pickup off. "I'll carry everything in, if you want to go in and check things out. All right?"

"Okay," she said, not going to try to figure out whether he was trying to baby her because she had cancer, or whether he was just being a gentleman.

She didn't have to question everything and figure out the why of things.

And sometimes, maybe he just did things without the why behind them, without thinking about it or having an angle. She was always trying to figure out people's angles. Even though she didn't always have an angle of her own. Because she didn't. Sometimes she did things just because.

It was not unreasonable to think that Mav did the same.

"Is it locked?" she asked as she got out of the pickup, figuring she would have to wait for him to walk in and unlock it.

"Nope. Never lock it. Go right in."

She grinned to herself, not surprised, and walked to the house, stepping up the steps onto the porch, which wasn't tiny but big enough for a swing and two rocking chairs.

She smiled at the rocking chairs, figuring that was probably something his sisters had insisted that he needed, or his mother. It definitely didn't seem like something Mav would want on his front porch. She couldn't imagine him taking the time to sit in the rocking chairs and actually enjoy them.

Although, maybe she could imagine him sitting out there in the evening, watching the sun go down, tired after working all day, but unable to get his brain to stop.

She smiled at the idea.

She walked in, taking her shoes off at the door and looking around. It was sparse. A lamp and a recliner. No blankets, and she was glad she had kept the basket back. Because, especially during the long North Dakota winter, she loved to snuggle in blankets and cuddle up in their warmth.

But being that there was only one recliner in the living room, they were going to need some of her furniture. There was room for her couch, or she could just bring her chair.

She wasn't sure which would be best, and she figured she and Mav could talk about it, although she couldn't imagine him having a strong feeling one way or the other.

Walking through the living room into the kitchen, she opened a couple cupboard doors and realized that Mav was not joking. They were basically bare. One cupboard had a stack of paper plates, but there were actually no real plates at all, and she was glad that she had decided to bring hers.

There was silverware in the silverware drawer, but just two of each piece, and there were some dirty dishes in the sink, which included two forks and two spoons. So it looked like he had a set of four.

She had brought her silverware too, so that was good.

Spices, pantry staples, plastic containers, bowls, measuring spoons. There wasn't any of that stuff. She laughed and shook her head. A true bachelor's pad.

Wandering back through the home, she saw two smaller bedrooms and a bath to share between them, and she poked her head into the master bedroom.

The bed was made, which kind of surprised her, but maybe he had done it thinking she would be coming. Mav seemed like the kind of person who threw back the covers and jumped into his day, never stopping to look behind him to see that there might be something that he needed to tidy up. Like he would want to be bothered with tidying anything up.

She supposed that trait might start to bother her after they'd been married for a while, but it made her smile now. Just thinking that they were so different. Because she went through her day, slowly and methodically, always taking time to tidy up behind her, washing the dishes when she was done with them, not letting them sit in the sink and pile up. She'd rather have just a few dishes to wash than a whole sink full.

The floor didn't seem excessively dirty, so either he swept for her arrival, or it hadn't been long since he swept. Of course, if he took his boots off before he came in, the house wouldn't get very messy.

"What do you think?" he asked, startling her, and she yanked her head out of the bedroom.

"I was just thinking it looked like you swept recently."

"Yeah. I think the day that we got married, I swept. That's been less than a week." He grinned. "Sometimes it goes for a while, especially in the summer when things get busy."

"If you take your boots off before you walk in, that probably keeps a lot of the dirt out."

"It does. I figured that out, and it's a little bit of extra work, but it saves me time."

"I'm surprised you don't have a dog. I expected you to."

"I've been meaning to get one. I just, even after I bought this place, I went trucking on the ice roads in the winters and did some fishing in Alaska as well."

"You're a sucker for punishment."

"I'll say. You think it's cold in North Dakota. You don't want to be on a fishing boat in the winter, with waves crashing up and ice forming on everything."

"Sounds pretty if you don't have to work in it."

"Have you ever seen the ocean?"

"No. I haven't. I guess... I guess I don't have a deep desire to see it either. Mom lives in California, and while she doesn't live next to the ocean, I'm sure we could visit it when I visit her if I wanted to."

"I kind of forgot about your mom. How is she? Did you tell her about the wedding?"

"She's fine. And, no. I didn't." She sighed. "That's probably me being a coward, because I know I'm going to take flack from her because she didn't know about it. But... I didn't either, really. And then there's going to be a stressful conversation, and I just...didn't want to go into it with her. I'm sorry. I'm a terrible daughter."

"I understand. Sometimes some parents make it hard to be a kid and for you to want to talk to them. When they demand so much out of you, it's exhausting to make a phone call to them."

"Your parents don't seem like they would be like that?"

"They're not. My mom is awesome, and she married a really great man. He's got a lot of wisdom, and I've learned things from him. Not necessarily from him lecturing me over the years, but just by watching. He's quiet, but his life speaks loud. One of those."

"Wow. That's great. You lucked out in the parent department."

"Yeah. Or God blessed me. Maybe because he knew I needed it. I needed a lot of direction because I have a tendency to take the wrong road."

"I hardly doubt that He gave me less, because He thought I didn't need as much. I'm not sure what to say about that, but it's funny that you know about how hard parents can make being a kid sometimes."

"I had buddies like that. They dreaded calling their folks because their folks always gave them a hard time. It wasn't a relaxing, fun phone call, it was an inquisition and a guilt trip, an 'I can't get off the phone fast enough' kind of thing. So, a lot of time would elapse between phone calls, and I'd feel bad for their parents, but if they would just learn to talk to their kids a little better. I... I want to say in a more fun way, but it's not that. Just be less judgmental, I guess. Once your kids are raised, there's really not much you can do besides sit back and hold on. They're not going to listen to you, especially if you browbeat them. So, you're better off not. But that's just my opinion. It might not be the right one."

"No. It sounds good. I think that would be something I need to keep in mind, if I ever—" She stopped abruptly. If she had children.

She was standing in front of his bedroom. And this was not exactly a conversation that she wanted to have with him right now. She felt a little off balance, and maybe it was something that everybody else talked about with ease, but she'd never exactly had a conversation like that before. Her face felt like it was on fire.

"I'm done looking at the house. I can help carry things in."

"Hey." He reached down, touching her arm, not grabbing a hold of it or forcing her to stop, but putting a little pressure on it. "I'm sorry. Whatever I said that was wrong, I'm sorry."

She needed to breathe. She was overreacting. This was ridiculous. She was a grown woman, and she could talk about children, about her children, and his children, their children together, and not get so embarrassed that she had to run away.

"It's me. I... I guess I started thinking about children. And realized that my children would also be yours, ours, and," she took a breath, "I'm standing in front of your bedroom, and it just felt weird. I'm an idiot sometimes. I'm sorry."

"You're an idiot?" He was smiling.

"You don't need to say that like I'm really an idiot," she snapped.

"You're not an idiot," he said, putting a hand on her one cheek and another hand on the other and tilting her head up gently to face him so that she was looking up at him. "You're not an idiot." He laughed. "That's not very romantic. Let me see if I can think of something else."

She waited.

Waited a little more.

Finally she said, "Don't strain yourself." She rolled her eyes, joking.

He laughed. "Stop making fun of me. I was trying to think of something really romantic, something that would knock you off your feet, but I'm coming up empty. All I can think of is you're beautiful, and you're amazing, and you've probably been told that a million times by a million different guys, and I'm just one of many."

"No. You're not. I haven't, and you're definitely not one of many, you're..." She wanted to say the only one, but she couldn't get the words to come out.

"I saw something on your phone. Something... Something I don't think I should have seen, but when you gave me your password..."

"Yeah?" Her stomach flipped. She wasn't sure what he was going to say, but she was afraid it would be something...hard.

Emotional.

And she wanted that hardness, she wanted that emotional connection with him, wanted the closeness and the bonding and to feel loved and cherished, but suddenly she was afraid, too.

She wasn't sure what she was afraid of, but she held her breath.

"The text said something about you marrying the person you'd had a crush on for years. Finally. Something like that. I... I clicked off it, because I wasn't really supposed to be reading it, but it stuck in my brain, and I've been wanting to ask you about it." He took a breath. Almost as though he were gathering his own courage. "Who have you had a crush on all your life?"

Chapter 23

"You."

Cassie's reply was soft, a whisper, and said with a little hesitation. She couldn't lie, didn't want to. She wanted Mav to know, mostly. She didn't think he was the kind of person who would lord it over her, laugh at the fool she'd been, or make fun of her because she was the one who had loved him for years and years.

"Really? You liked me?"

She nodded. "Forever."

He shook his head. "I can't even begin to imagine."

"No, I know. You never noticed me. It's okay."

"Because I was stupid."

"No. Not at all. You just... I'm not the kind of person that people notice. Most of the time, I don't want to be noticed. Even right now, with all of your attention on me, it makes me nervous."

He grinned a little, his mouth curving up. "This makes you nervous?"

His amusement made her smile. Of course he wasn't going to let her get away with saying that. And she shouldn't. There was no reason for her to be anxious or upset, except she seemed to be wired that way. Maybe it was the cancer that had done it to her, that made her anxious about forming attachments, when she never knew when she would be leaving, and she didn't want to hurt anyone.

"A little," she said. "I'm not going to let you scare me away."

He grinned wider. His thumb skimmed across her cheekbone.

"I waited too long for this," she added, trying to make her brain work, even though her eyes wanted to close.

"That's crazy. I couldn't find a single woman in all of Sweet Water who wanted to have anything to do with me, and you stepped out, and I couldn't believe it. And now I find out that this is how you felt all along." His face crinkled. "What took you so long to step out?"

"I told the Lord I wasn't going to chase you. That I was going to give you up. That it seemed like I had wasted a lot of time, and that if you weren't something that He was going to give to me, then I wasn't going to keep hoping and dreaming. I wasn't going to spend any more mental energy on you."

"But that still doesn't really explain why you took a chance on me and stepped out to the aisle."

"I thought there would be a whole pile of people, women, tripping over themselves to get to you. I... That wasn't what I promised. I told the Lord I wasn't going to fight and scratch. But when eleven thirty came and no one had volunteered, it wasn't like I was fighting and scratching anymore, it was like God had the door open, and I just needed to walk through. So I did."

"Man, I'm going to do everything in my power to make sure you don't regret that decision." His thumb moved along her cheekbone, and his hands threaded in her hair. He pulled her closer, and she went willingly, putting her arms around his waist, hardly able to believe that she was finally standing here in Mav's embrace, the embrace she'd dreamed about for years.

"I don't want to destroy whatever we have here, but you talked about children. I hadn't been sure whether you'd be able to have any or not. Are you?"

"The doctors couldn't say for sure. Maybe."

She held her breath. Mav had struck her as the kind of man who would absolutely want to have children, and maybe it was something they should have talked about before they got married. They just...got married fast.

"I'm sorry I didn't mention it before the wedding. It was a quick one. And I suppose I didn't have time."

"No. It's okay. Whatever God gives us is what we'll take, and I'll be grateful for them."

She couldn't say anything. Her heart was too full.

"I know we have a lot of things to do, but I was wondering if it would be okay if I kiss you?"

"I was hoping you would." Her answer was simple. It was the truth. She wanted him to, had been hoping since the moment she stepped into his embrace that he wasn't just going to hug her like a friend and let her go.

"Can I admit I'm a little nervous? I mean, that's a lot of years of dreaming, and I'm pretty sure I'm not going to live up to it. No one has ever complimented me on my kissing skills."

"And you've kissed a lot of women?" She wanted to close her mouth over those words. They probably were words that she shouldn't ask, but...he was her husband. She should know, shouldn't she?

"Less than you think. Most of the time, my relationships have been short and I would say sweet, but that would be a lie. Short and rocky. Short and abruptly over, with me being confused as to why. I... I think I might have some idea, but I'm hoping you'll help me, because I'm planning on this relationship lasting for the rest of my life, and I'm hoping you are too."

"I am. For sure. I wouldn't have gone into it thinking anything else."

His head came down, and he brushed a kiss on her temple. "Have I ever mentioned how good you smell?" he murmured as his lips moved down and kissed her cheek.

"I'm not sure."

"I'm sorry. I don't have all the pretty words. I wish I did. You deserve them."

"I just want the true ones," she said, knowing that was the truth. She didn't want pretty words that weren't true. She didn't want a bunch of platitudes that were just designed to get her to do whatever he wanted her to do. She wanted the truth. Just the true words. The honest ones. The heart words. Those were the ones that she would cherish. Not the ones that didn't feel right or accurate or the ones that felt like they were made up and told to a hundred different women in a hundred different ways.

"You make me feel things I've never felt before. I have never been nervous and eager and excited and crazy infatuated like this before. I admire you, respect you, and as much as I want to emulate your walk with the Lord, I also have a lot more fleshly feelings, which are weird in a way, but feel so right."

"I think... I think I need to say thank you."

"You don't have to. I'm just telling you. It's not words wrapped up in a pretty bow, just the truth." He kissed the side of her lips, and she closed her eyes, moving her mouth just a little bit until their lips met, and she smiled, because that was what she wanted.

Maybe he smiled a little too, and their teeth scraped together, which made her giggle, which made him hold her tighter, which she appreciated, because she was feeling a little dizzy as his mouth settled down on hers and he deepened the kiss, and while it was a little awkward, it was also better than anything she had dreamed of or could imagine, and she didn't want it to ever end.

She had to pull back, to breathe, to suck in air, although she wouldn't have minded standing there in the hall practicing kissing for a really long time, but he leaned his forehead against hers, his breath just as ragged as hers, and he smiled.

"That wasn't too bad. I wouldn't mind doing that a few more times."

"Not too bad? I'm not sure that's a very good testament to my kissing skills. In fact, I think it's more of a nod to my ineptness."

"No. If there's anyone who's inept, it's me. But I'll take all the blame for being inept, as long as you let me continue to practice."

"I'm all about practicing," she said. "But I suppose we ought to be responsible adults and finish moving me into your house before we get sidetracked in the hallway."

"Your practicality is one of the things I really love about you, but right now, I wish you were just as flighty as I am, because I'm totally willing to quit working and just kiss for the rest of the day."

"Just kiss?" She lifted her brows and wondered if her fumbling attempt at flirting was going to be met with shock or surprise.

She should have known he would laugh.

"That's tempting."

"Really?" she asked, wiggling her brows like that had been her intention.

"You're teasing me."

"Oh. I thought that's what you were doing with me. After all, I'm the one who's had a crush for fifteen years."

"That long?"

"I don't know. Since I was fifteen probably. Maybe not quite."

"Hopefully we'll have a lot longer than that to practice," he said, straightening and seeming to be reluctant to let her go.

She loved the idea that he didn't want to let go of her and that he wanted to keep holding her.

"I hope so," she said, and she pushed the idea of cancer and all that to the back of her mind. She didn't have any control over that, and she wasn't going to worry about it. She was just thrilled that her husband seemed to be enamored of her, and she couldn't ask for more.

"So, I have an idea," Mav said, straightening up and backing away from her.

"Okay," she said, falling into step with him as he walked back down the hall.

"How about we work until four, and then we'll quit and take a ride."

"A car ride, right?" she asked, wondering where in the world they would drive to.

"A horse ride. We'll see the ranch. I'll show it to you. I'm actually kind of excited about it. It's been something I've been thinking about for a while, but I know that we've been busy."

"All right." And she was proud of herself. She didn't say no, she didn't even mumble the word but immediately said yes.

"You said yes," Mav said, grabbing a hold of her hand and lifting it to his lips and kissing it.

It made her tingle clear to her toes, and it also made her feel like the kiss maybe wasn't a mistake. He had enjoyed it as much as she had. She was pretty sure about that anyway.

That and the fact that he noticed that she was keeping her word and doing what she said she was going to try to do, which was say yes.

"All right, it's a deal. Riding after work."

"Sounds good."

Chapter 24

"This is Sunshine, and she's sweet," Mav said as he led his pretty little mare over to Cassie, who looked a little nervous.

"It's a girl?" she asked, lifting her chin. He loved that little tell that she was trying to be brave.

He hadn't really meant to ask her to go riding to scare her.

He hadn't meant that at all. He wanted to do it as something that they could enjoy together. A reward for the hard work they were doing. And another way to spend time with her, doing something he was comfortable with.

He didn't mind helping her pack up her house or moving her into his. He figured he ought to. And if he really hated it, he could have made a phone call and had five or ten of his siblings helping them within an hour.

They would have done whatever he asked them to do, he knew it, just as they knew they could count on him for the same.

But he hadn't wanted to. Which was unusual for him, because normally he didn't mind a crowd. But he wanted to spend time alone with Cassie. Time for them to get to know each other. Or maybe he just enjoyed the way she looked at him, the way they talked together, the conversations they had, and the way she made him laugh. He didn't want to give that up.

So, he hadn't made the call, hadn't even suggested it.

Cassie, being an only child, probably hadn't even thought to ask, or maybe she was just the kind of person that didn't like to bother people.

That would be something he could see in her as well.

Regardless, he was glad, because if they had had people helping them, they would still be working, and he wouldn't be out in the barn, by himself, with his wife.

"She's a girl, and she's the calmest horse I have. In fact, she's so calm it's kind of hard to get her to even walk, and she definitely doesn't go faster than that without a lot of encouragement from someone."

"All right. How do I get from here to there," she said, nodding from where she was up into the saddle.

"You gotta put your foot in the stirrup, your left foot, and you're going to grab a hold of the pommel, then jump and pull yourself up. It's kind of a learned technique, so nobody's expecting you to be graceful at it today, but go ahead, unless you want me to help you." He couldn't help it, his voice dropped a little on those last few words, and they sounded like an invitation. As well they should, since if it was an excuse to touch her, he would take it.

He couldn't remember ever being this besotted with someone. Which he supposed was a good thing, since he was married to her. And she had a crush on him.

But even with this crush, the crush that she said she had, she seemed a little surprised that there was kissing involved. And definitely a little uncomfortable at anything else that might be involved. So, he wasn't giving himself any grand ideas of his wife wanting all the things that he wanted, and even if she did, he still wanted to woo her. To do all the things that a man did for the woman that he loved.

He'd never wanted that before either. In most of his relationships, all of them, it had been all about him and what he wanted. Maybe that had more to do with what he had talked to the Lord about not that long ago, or maybe it had to do with Cassie and how unselfish she was. It made him want to be the same.

"All right, so that means you're not going to laugh at me?"

"I didn't say that."

"Great."

He laughed.

"How about you go get on your horse, and I'll work on getting on mine... This kind of looks pretty high, and I'm not sure I can do it."

"I know you can do it, and I'm not going anywhere. I want to make sure I can catch you if you fall. I'm not expecting you to, but it would be kind of irresponsible of me for me to take you for your first ride and not even stick around to make sure you got on her okay."

"All right. Far be it for me to insult your teaching abilities, on your very first lesson on my very first ride."

"I'm glad you see I have a reputation to establish."

She grinned at him, and he kept a hold on Sunshine's bridle, standing to the side so he had one arm free to help Cassie if she needed it.

But she gritted her teeth, grabbed a hold of her saddle horn, put her foot in the stirrup, and to his surprise, she didn't hop on exactly, but she made it on okay.

"You're more coordinated than I am. It took me forever to get the hang of that. And I started when I was a kid."

"Well, maybe it was just beginner's luck," she said, and his lips quirked.

"You're always humble. You know, you can admit that you're good at things."

She sighed. "Maybe that was another lesson of the cancer, but I kind of feel like every breath I take is just because of God. So, I can say that I'm good, and I might joke about it, but really, I know that everything I have comes from the Lord. I'm so aware of that. I don't even know why. But my breath, if I have balance, if I do good work, my graphic design business, and..." She looked down at him. "Here I am married to you. That was nothing short of the Lord's hand working in my life. I would never in a million years have thought that this was the way things were going to turn out. But He gave me what I wanted. It's interesting that He only did it after I let go."

"Yeah. That is interesting. I wonder if that's a test of some sort, that you passed. Not that I feel like I'm a great reward, but I feel like sometimes we hold so tightly to things that we don't really realize that we don't need them until we let them go."

"Yeah. Only, it wasn't that I realized I didn't need you, it was just that I realized I needed God more. I suppose it took me a long time to learn that lesson, but it's the truth. As much as I love living here and love being married to you and can't wait for and look forward to our life together, I know that I need God more."

"I suppose there are parts of my male vanity that are a little bit offended, but it actually makes me feel pretty secure to know that my wife has such a firm connection with the Creator. Like, I'm married to someone who has a special 'in' with God."

"Like you need it?" She raised a brow, and he knew she was joking.

"You know I do."

He told her how to hold the reins in her hands, and there wasn't much adjustment, she seemed almost like a natural. And then he said, "Sunshine should just stand there. I'm going to go get on Richard, and we'll start out."

He probably should have kept her in the paddock for her first ride. But Sunshine really was dependable and pretty much im-placable. She never bolted or got scared; he'd never seen it. And he'd had all of his nieces and nephews on her at some point. She carried a lot of kids around, and he'd trust her with anyone, or he wouldn't have put his wife on her back.

He realized that her safety and welfare were becoming more and more important to him.

He supposed that was a natural thing, maybe something that a lot of people felt even before they were married, but he never really thought that. Of course, working on a boat crew, he had a concern for his crewmates, but nothing like this. Even the feeling that he had for his sisters and his mom couldn't compare.

Nor should it.

He supposed God had made man and woman to leave their families and cleave to each other, creating a family unit of their own. Something strong and unbreakable, and to do that, men needed to feel this way about their wives.

Funny that a lot of men didn't.

Maybe they bought into the narcissistic culture that he had. Where it was always me first, where a man put his needs before everyone else's needs and took care of himself.

He didn't want to be that way, and he was blessed to have a wife who seemed to be patient enough to wait for him to make mistakes and learn from them.

Chapter 25

"**I** never expected it to be so much fun!" Cassie said, knowing her cheeks were bright and her eyes full of excitement.

They had just gotten back to the ranch from driving Cord's Percheron team, and she had to admit she'd fallen in love. Not just with Ben and Gus, his horses, but with sitting in the driver seat and holding the reins, and being the one to call the shots.

She'd loved every second of it.

"I never expected you to be so natural at it. You just don't seem like the type, but you sure surprised me. You are amazing."

Mav smiled at her, and she glowed, maybe not entirely from the horses but also from the look in his eye. The way he made her feel when he looked at her that way. It made her want to step over and put her arms around him, tug his head down, and convince him to kiss her again.

It was Wednesday. They'd ridden on Monday afternoon, but they worked straight through on Tuesday, pushing to have everything done on Wednesday so they could go to Cord's and practice driving the team.

She also got some work in, while he had some work outside to do.

He had promised he would help her make the chicken that he'd learned how to make on Sunday at the cooking class, and then she was going to take it in and deliver it to Miss June who had just gotten out of the hospital, while he did the work that needed to be done in the field. They were going to make a double batch, so there was enough for them to eat that evening for supper.

All of her things had been moved, and the only stuff that was left were a couple of pieces of furniture, including her couch, that they were going to move into his house and some things to take to the secondhand drop-off.

Mav had some of his brothers coming Thursday morning to help with that furniture, and they'd already contacted a real estate agent to put her house up for sale. They would be coming Thursday to take pictures, once Cassie had cleaned it.

It had been a long, hard week, and it was only half over. She was exhausted, but she was also having so much fun. Knowing Mav, and being with him, had added so much color and sparkle to her life, she could hardly believe the difference.

She supposed she'd get used to being married to him, and what felt so new and amazing now would eventually feel like her new normal, but that thought made her happy too. Because she loved the life that they had together and looked forward to it feeling normal.

If only they would hear from the lawyer. It'd only been a few days, but that seemed to be the cloud that hung over them.

That, and her feeling like they had a strong enough relationship to move to the next level.

Mav hadn't said any more, and he hadn't been pushing to kiss her.

She wasn't sure if that was out of respect for her, or because he didn't want to.

His seeming lack of interest had made her insecure.

Maybe he hadn't enjoyed the kisses as much as he claimed. Although he did seem to enjoy spending time with her. Maybe that was only because he felt like he had to.

She tried not to allow her mind to dwell on those thoughts. If that was the truth, then she would just have to face it, but she didn't have to torture herself with the idea that maybe her husband wasn't attracted to her.

Because of the money, she probably didn't have to worry about him divorcing her. Or leaving her. They would have to pay it back if that happened, and he definitely wouldn't want to do that. So he would do everything in his power to stay with her. Still, if he wasn't attracted to her, she wasn't sure she wanted to stay together.

Except marriage was for life, so whatever she got, she was going to work with. Whatever she had to do.

"You ready to make chicken?" he asked, coming up beside her and putting his arm around her.

She didn't think she would ever get tired of that. She often longed for the touch of someone, someone to hold her and cuddle with. Maybe touch was a love language for her, she wasn't sure. But whatever it was, when he put his arm around her, she always wanted to lean into his side and just get closer.

She resisted the urge. "I thought you were doing it yourself?"

"No. Miss Jane taught me, so I can teach you. Next time, you can do it all by yourself."

"While the king of the castle sits on the couch with his feet propped up?"

"You know me, always sitting around on the couch." He looked tellingly at the spot where there was no couch.

"Soon. Soon we'll have a couch, so the king of the castle can sit there."

"I don't think I want to sit on the couch without you," he said casually as he walked into the kitchen, and she trailed along after him, bemused. Funny how one little sentence from him could make her feel warm and gooey inside.

She should be getting used to it by now, but he had the ability to discombobulate her with his casual comments that obviously meant a lot more to her than they did to him.

She tried not to worry about that. It was probably normal for a woman to be more emotional and a man to be more casual. She had to tell herself that.

They got the chicken out, and she was kind of impressed that he actually remembered how to do it, just from reading a card that Jane had given him.

It wasn't any time at all before they had the chicken made for their supper and enough to put in a casserole dish for her to take to June to warm up for her supper.

She had heard June was doing fairly well and figured while she was there she would offer to see if there was any housework she could do.

"Are you sure you're going to be okay without me?" she asked, not because she thought he wouldn't be, but because she really didn't want to leave, and she was dragging her feet about it.

"You know, I've gotten used to you hanging around all the time, and I think I'm going to miss you."

"I'm definitely going to miss you. It's kinda crazy how much I enjoy your company. But I do."

Her words had made him feel good. She could tell by the glow on his face, and to her surprise, he put an arm around her back and leaned down, giving her a kiss, quick but firm.

She really didn't want it to be so fast, but she steadied herself as he pulled away and said, "You be careful, okay?"

"I'm just driving to town. I'll be fine."

"I'm serious. I don't want anything to happen to you."

"That's just because it's so hard to find a wife. Especially when you announce in the morning that you want to get married that night."

"Are you going to tease me about that forever? Or just like for the next fifty years?"

"Oh, forever. For sure." She grinned. "I'll be careful. And you be careful too. I can't believe how attached I've become to you in just a short week. It's true that we spent pretty much every waking hour together, and now we have to separate, which feels harder than it should."

"I know. You're just going into town. I'll see you for supper, but I want to trail after you, almost like a puppy, and whine for you to take me with you. But I know I have work to do."

"I do too. When I get back, I'm going to have to get started on it. I probably won't have it done by supper, so I'll need to work this evening too."

"No problem. Wherever you are, I'll just lie down at your feet and put my head on your toes or something."

"All right. That might be a little bit much."

"Really. You think?"

They smiled at each other, and he was waiting for her to turn and open the door so he could carry the casserole to her car, but instead of turning, she stepped closer, tugging on his head and bringing it down.

She kissed him like she wanted him to kiss her, and she wasn't sure exactly how he felt about it, other than he made a noise that sounded like a groan, and that made her smile.

She pulled her head back. "Now that's a proper goodbye kiss."

"Warn me next time, because I don't want to be holding a casserole and not be able to put my arms around you. That was like torture."

"All right. We both have a learning curve. I think we can do this. You kiss me properly next time, and I'll make sure that you're not holding a casserole while you do it."

He laughed. "I'm not sure that's exactly what I meant, but practicing, I'm on it."

He helped her out to the car, putting the casserole on the seat beside her and standing and watching her while she backed up and pulled away.

She rode to town with a grin on her face. It was a silly grin, one of those teenage I'm infatuated with my boyfriend kind of grins. Only she was an adult, and she was married to the object of her infatuation. And he'd been her crush for years.

She reached June's house and walked around the car to carry the casserole in.

Just June's car was parked next to the house, and so she assumed that her husband must still be working.

She had heard in town that June had been discharged from the hospital and someone else had to take her home, because her husband was helping the neighbor lady with something.

Cassie wasn't sure whether that was true or not, but if it was, her heart went out to June. She had known that June and Miss Helen were both having issues in their marriage, and Miss April, who had been married for over fifty years, was helping them a bit at the community center at times.

That had spilled over into helping other people with their marriages and had been a real blessing around Sweet Water, from what Cassie had heard.

Still, it must be hard to have a husband who neglected his wife so badly.

She tried to imagine what her relationship would be like in thirty years, but she couldn't. Would Mav and she grow apart? She didn't want that to happen. She would try with all her heart not to allow it to. She didn't want to become another statistic. Someone who lost their marriage and was just one more divorce on the tally.

Walking up the steps, she knocked on the door, but then she opened it slowly and called out, "Hello! I'm coming in, so you don't have to get up," as she walked in and closed the door.

"We're in here," a voice that did not sound like June said.

"I'm sorry. I didn't realize you had company."

"Not company, just Helen and me. We usually hang out at the community center and do some crafting, but with June laid up, we figured we'd come here for the day. She seems like she enjoyed the company, and she's a little more perky than she had been a few days ago."

"Good. I brought supper," Cassie said, stopping in the doorway. "I'm going to go in and set it on the stove. It'll be ready to warm up in the oven whenever you want. It's already cooked."

"Thank you," June said, sounding a little weak but not completely terrible.

Cassie walked back and stepped in the doorway of the living room. "I thought I would offer to do any sweeping or dusting or cleaning that you needed. Your sink was empty, so you don't have any dishes to do."

"No. April and Helen have taken care of me." June sat on the couch, propped up by pillows, her legs up beside her, and her arms in her lap.

Fatigue lined her face, but she didn't seem to be in great pain. Still, she wasn't moving very fast.

"You can come on in and visit for a spell," Miss June said. "I wanted to know how your marriage is going."

"It's going well. We're kind of adjusting. I think that kind of thing is always an adjustment. But Mav is a great guy, he makes me laugh, but he's trying to do right too. And I admire that."

"Has he kissed you yet?" Miss April asked.

Cassie supposed at Miss April's age, she could get away with a question like that.

Cassie didn't like to talk about details of her personal life much at all. When she had cancer, it was all she could do to tell people the details of her treatment. It made them feel included and gave them a direction, to know how to pray for her.

But she kind of liked keeping things close to her. Especially whatever it was going on between Mav and her. It felt soft and tender and exciting, and just something that she wanted to keep close to her.

But June was recovering from surgery and facing cancer treatments down the road. She also was struggling in her marriage, and the culmination of all those things would be enough to make any woman feel depressed.

Maybe hearing about Cassie's marriage might help June smile a little bit.

So she said, "He has. And it was pretty amazing."

"Better than your dreams?" Miss April asked, seeming to know that she had crushed on Mav for years.

"Much better." She smiled. Better because there was an actual man in front of her. Not that Mav had any kind of standard to live up to. Because it didn't really matter how he kissed her. It would have been perfect, because it was Mav.

"I think probably how a man kisses doesn't really matter. It's what kind of character he has. But I think we always like to hear about the kissing," Miss April said with a knowing look.

That had been exactly what Cassie had been thinking, and she nodded. "I agree. He is a lot more mature than the town gives him credit for. I think it bothers him that he has a reputation to try to live down, and he's discouraged, because it seems like everybody always throws up all the youthful things that he used to do in his face, and he feels like it doesn't matter what he does, no one's ever going to notice that he isn't that person anymore."

"That would have to be discouraging. I've never thought about that. But I suppose we do kind of hold people to the reputation that they had when they were a kid. You never really outlive it."

"No. And that's the reason a good reputation is very hard to build and a bad reputation is easy to 'earn.'"

"I don't think kids understand that. They don't realize how careful they have to be with the things that they do, that those things are going to follow them for all their lives, and they'll never live them down. So they need to watch their step."

"I certainly never thought that when I was a teenager. But I guess I wanted to please my mom. I wanted to make her proud of me, which never seemed to happen, but I would strive for that. So I guess I avoided some of the pitfalls that other people fell into."

"It's very mature of you to look past Mav's reputation and see the man that he has become." Miss Helen paused. "Did you know that before you stepped down the aisle? Or is that something you figured out in the last week or so?"

"I've been watching him for a long time. I guess I can admit that, because he knows that I've had a crush on him for years. Over a decade even. And, yeah. I knew that he was more mature, that there was more to him than what people gave him credit for. I guess I didn't just watch what he said or he did, but I watched his facial expressions, body language, what he did when other people weren't looking at him and he wasn't the center of attention."

"Well, that's a good way to scope out a potential husband. And then somehow have him ask for a bride, and be the one to step out."

Cassie smiled. They had no idea about the money. And she certainly wasn't going to tell them. It definitely was the Lord who had orchestrated that, and she wasn't going to argue with Him or however He worked things. But still, she didn't have to tell all of her secrets either.

"All right. I think I'd better head home. I have a job to do, and I have a husband to get supper for. Although it's already made, all I have to do is warm mine up too."

"Maybe he'll come in and warm it up for you, if you're working."

"He just might. That wouldn't surprise me at all."

Chapter 26

Later that night, after she'd worked all afternoon, and they'd eaten the chicken together, and he cleaned up the dishes while she went back to work, Cassie stretched and looked at the clock.

It was one thirty AM. She had lost herself in her project and hadn't realized it was so late.

Mav, true to his word, lay on the floor at her feet while she sat in his chair.

They needed to get their couch in here.

She should have made him go to bed hours ago, but she hadn't, and now, she looked at him lying on the floor, Phyllis snuggled up in his arms.

He cradled the dog gently, even in his sleep, and he snored lightly, lying on his back with one of her shoes as a pillow.

She stared at him for a bit, admiring the long slope of his nose, the curve of his lips, which of course made her shiver just a bit, but he wasn't watching, and she could study them. Funny how lips could feel so good on hers. Just looking at them could bring back those memories and make her want to kneel down and touch his with hers.

She didn't want to wake him. He'd had a hard day. He always worked hard. Was always busy. Always finding something to do.

And yet, there he was with her dog, snuggled up, with Mav holding her carefully, even though it was funny to see a man like Mav with a little dog like Phyllis.

He needed some kind of strong, mangy mutt running beside him. Following him around the farm, chasing groundhogs and prairie dogs and helping him with the cattle. Whatever it was that farm dogs did.

But he'd taken to hers, and Phyllis trusted him, and despite them looking odd together, they enjoyed each other's company, and Phyllis even sought him out.

Closing her laptop, she stretched her shoulders, cracking her neck from side to side, before she carefully put the recliner part of the chair down and slid slowly to her feet.

Setting her computer on the table, she grabbed two of the pillows that she'd brought from her house.

Carefully moving her shoe out from underneath Mav's head, she replaced it with a pillow. His breathing hitched and she froze, but then it resumed. And she finished putting the pillow under him. Phyllis didn't move at all.

Grabbing a blanket, she spread it out over top of him, and then, not sure if she was being maybe a little presumptuous, she knelt down, lifted the blanket, and crawled underneath it, curving her legs to match his while she put her head on his arm and her arm around his waist. If he noticed that she was now snuggled next to him, his snoring didn't stop, and he didn't move.

So she assumed she hadn't even woken him.

Whatever he did, he did with all his heart, whether it was working, or cooking, or sleeping.

She smiled at the thought. He flung himself into whatever he did, and she hoped that included marriage.

Still smiling, she squeezed a little, pressing herself against his side and closing her eyes.

She thought she might lie awake for a while, getting used to this new idea of sleeping beside a man, but before she knew it, the world had gone black, and all she knew was the warmth of the man beside her.

Chapter 27

Mav woke suddenly. He figured it was probably three AM or so. The normal time. Stiff. He felt weighed down.

He tried to move his arm but found it heavy.

Moving his hand around, he felt hair, lots of hair. Then he remembered that he'd fallen asleep on the floor while Cassie had been working. Phyllis had been in his arms, and he thought the warm body of the dog was what he felt.

But there was something on his other side.

Not sure whether to be annoyed or grateful that Cassie hadn't woken him up when she had gone to bed, he realized that she'd put a blanket over him. But there was still something else.

He moved his head, and his chin brushed...hair?

He sniffed.

He would recognize her scent anywhere. Even in the dark, on the floor, in his living room.

He grinned. She hadn't gone to bed without him. But she had gone to bed without waking him up. She had covered him, which was kind of her, because he knew specifically that he hadn't had a blanket. He actually used her shoe as a pillow.

How sad was that?

But as he moved his head, he realized it wasn't her shoe under his head anymore. It was a pillow. But more than that, it was the woman beside him. Cassie had not left him, she'd joined him.

He couldn't remember the last time he'd woken up smiling like that.

Her legs were all entangled with his, and her arm was around his waist. She held onto him tightly, like she didn't want him to leave her, and if she were awake, he would have assured her that he definitely was not leaving.

His two ladies. Phyllis on one side and Cassie on the other. Of course, Cassie was kind of the big deal, since Phyllis wasn't exactly choosy about who she lay around with.

Having Cassie beside him was a true blessing.

She wasn't the kind of girl who would do this with just any man.

But he was her husband.

Of course, that didn't guarantee that she would do it with him either. He hadn't been sure. He'd been clear about what he wanted when they got married, but when he had told her that he would leave it up to her, he had meant it. Even if it took a lot longer than he wanted it to.

But she had trusted him enough to lie down beside him.

And, he assumed, she had known what she was doing when she snuggled up to him.

He pulled her closer, and she stirred a little, her hair moving under his nose and her legs moving with his.

He had his jeans on still, and so did she, but if this was a little taste of what married life would be like, he was definitely in for it.

He smiled, and for the first time in a long time, he closed his eyes and went back to sleep.

Chapter 28

Ellen lifted Daisy's halter and scratched her cow under her neck.

Her friends had gone to visit family out of town, and they wouldn't be in the parade with her. She'd be walking Daisy by herself.

She guessed she didn't really care, but it was always more fun to do things with friends.

Still, she had told Miss Charlene that she would walk Daisy in the parade route, and she had to keep her word.

Uncle Tadgh wouldn't allow her to do anything different, and at her age, although she was just thirteen, she wanted to be responsible, someone people could trust. So, she was going to do what she said she was going to do.

Her eyes were caught on Travis, who walked around the corner of the auction barn where the parade was setting up.

They'd go through Sweet Water and end at the Powers' trucking company on the other end of town.

It would be a long walk, but she and Daisy would enjoy it. Daisy loved the attention, and it helped her uncle sell his Highlanders too. People could see how gentle they were, that even a child could lead one in the parade.

But the sight of Travis made her slightly less eager. She hadn't thought he'd be here. He'd been working pretty hard for Mr. Hansen, and while she wouldn't have expected him to have to work on the Fourth of July, she also wouldn't have thought he would be in the parade.

Then she realized, he probably wasn't going to be in the parade. His eyes were caught on something, and she followed his gaze, realizing when she saw who he was looking at that he was just here to look at her.

Shanna.

The girl that Travis couldn't seem to take his eyes off of.

Ellen looked down at her own jeans and boots and T-shirt. It was a nice T-shirt, with flowers on it and a unicorn in one corner. And it was her favorite, because it was blue, with rainbow colors, and that appealed to her eyes and her senses, but it wasn't anything compared to what Shanna wore.

Ellen was old enough to know that guys liked girls who wore short skirts and midriff-showing outfits. And that's exactly what Shanna had on. Her tight top ended high enough to show a good six inches of her toned stomach.

She was here with the cheerleaders, and they would be doing formations as they did the parade route, and it would be a huge draw. People loved it.

Their outfits notwithstanding.

She castigated herself for still having feelings for someone who was so easily motivated by a little skin and less brains.

She said that in her head, and she knew it was catty as she tried to push the thought aside.

Shanna was just as smart as anyone else. Maybe she didn't do very well in school, but she was good at other things, and she had a nice figure, and that counted for a lot with men, it seemed.

Better than Ellen.

She didn't have to see herself in the mirror to know that she didn't really have any curves. She just had kind of a chunky belly, with legs that were padded and thick and straight.

Some girls had a little extra weight and carried it in such a way that it just accented their curves.

That was not her. She was just stout.

That's what Uncle Tadgh said sometimes.

A stout Irish girl.

Like that was a compliment.

She tried not to resent it because she knew Uncle Tadgh didn't mean it as an insult. He meant it as a compliment. But it wasn't something that she wanted to be. She wanted to be beautiful. Not stout.

She wanted to be curvy and...whatever the words were. Luscious?

Yeah. That sounded very enticing. If a man—Travis—looked at her and thought luscious, that was definitely good.

No one was going to look at her in her dirty boots, rainbow unicorn shirt, and worn blue jeans and think luscious. They were going to look at her and think stout.

She'd have to thank Uncle Tadgh for not lying to her.

She watched as Travis went over, and Shanna, who had to see him come, deliberately turned her back on him.

Ellen figured that it was probably not because she didn't want to talk to him, although it might be a little bit that, but it was more that she wanted him to have to work to get to her.

Ellen didn't typically employ feminine wiles, partly because she was stout, but also because she looked ridiculous when she tried to simper and act helpless.

Anyone who knew her knew she wasn't helpless.

She ran her hand down Daisy's neck, and Daisy turned her head, pushing her nose against Ellen, and that said to Ellen that she cared.

"Sometimes it feels like you're the only one, Daisy," she whispered, but she knew her words were dramatic. Even as a teenager, she had those tendencies, and she didn't want to be a drama queen.

So she tried to turn her head away, but she had to see if Shanna was going to talk to Travis.

He walked around, touching her arm, saying something to her.

Shanna rolled her eyes and said something that made the girls around her titter. It made Travis's cheeks heat.

They stood and talked for less than five minutes, but it felt like an eternity, and Ellen wished the parade would just get started already.

But it didn't, and while she managed to tear her eyes away, putting her arms over Daisy's back, leaning against her and scratching her at the same time, she was very aware that her crush on Travis was hopeless, and she should let him go, but she still fought the urge to keep watching to see what happened as he talked to Shanna.

"Hey there, kid," a voice said, and she started.

"Travis. Are you here? What a surprise. I thought you'd be working today."

She was ridiculous. No one was going to believe her when she said she was surprised to see him. She was surprised to see him beside *her*. That was true.

But at least maybe he wouldn't suspect that she'd been staring at him for the last five minutes.

"I saw you looking at me. I know you knew I was here," he said, laughing, walking over to the other side of Daisy, bending down so his face was in front of hers. "What's the matter? You look like you're down in the dumps."

"Just waiting for the parade to start. I've got work to do when I get home, so I'm ready to get in and get out so I can get started on my work."

"Oh? Big plans for tonight, something you have to get done so you can go on a big date or something?"

"I'm only thirteen. I don't date." She looked down her nose at him. Sometimes he was such a jerk, and she didn't know why she even liked him.

"Only thirteen? I thought you were older than that."

"That's just because I can outwork you." She narrowed her eyes, straightened, putting her hands across her chest, like she was protecting herself from him. She wasn't going to like him anymore. All he did was chase after that stupid Shanna, and he couldn't see how vapid she was. How she was just using him to get what she wanted. And how he was like a puppet at the end of a string, doing whatever she wanted.

"Wow. That's nice. I think that's Miss Cassie," Travis said, and the tone of his voice made Ellen straighten and turn around.

Sure enough, it was Miss Cassie sitting on the driver seat of what looked like Cord Stryker's carriage. His team of Percherons—Ben and Gus, if she wasn't mistaken—were pulling, all brushed with their amazing tails flowing in the wind, their harnesses jingling, and the carriage, the silver highlights shining in the sun, rolling along behind them effortlessly.

"Is that Mav in the back?" she asked.

"That's funny. They just got married. She's pulling her husband in the just married carriage. Except she's driving."

"I guess that's not a sight you see every day," she said, smiling and mostly forgetting her pique at him. They could be friends. She supposed they could. If she could control herself and remember that she wasn't allowed to have a crush on him, because he was just going to break her heart. Because he didn't want a girl like her, he wanted a girl like Shanna. Empty head and gorgeous body.

"Those horses are so pretty."

"Cord's been breeding them for years. I'm pretty sure both of those were born on his farm."

"How do you know that?"

"Uncle Tadgh is friends with them. He shoes them, too. It's quite a chore."

"I bet. I wouldn't want to get kicked by one of those."

"They're big, but they're very gentle. That's the hallmark of draft horses, their gentle disposition. Just like Highlanders." Ellen nodded at her cow.

Even as she did so, she was kicking herself. Boys didn't like girls who went around talking about how much they loved their cow.

"Daisy is pretty sweet. She has those big horns and she looks pretty ferocious, but she's just a big butterball."

"Butterball? If you're insulting my cow, I might have to call you on it."

"It was a compliment. Wasn't it, Daisy? You knew what I was saying," Travis said, giving Daisy's head a scratch.

Ellen tried not to pay attention to what he was doing. Tried not to smile at his words. Tried not to think how cute he was, scratching her cow.

She didn't want to like him.

After all, Shanna.

But it wasn't her nature to be mean, and she forgot her irritation as several kids ran over and asked if they could pet her. Knowing Daisy loved the attention, Ellen nodded at them and showed them where to scratch, the places Daisy liked the best. Under her neck, on her brisket, and under her legs.

"Is she going to hurt me?" one of the little ones asked.

"No. She's used to being touched all over, and she's used to all this commotion. In fact, she likes the attention."

"Cool!" the little kid said, scratching for a bit more before he ran off, yelling thank you over his shoulder.

"I think you like that just as much as your cow does," Travis said, watching the little kids run away before smirking at Ellen and petting Daisy a little bit more.

She noticed that he angled his body so that he could look up and see Shanna and her friends practicing their routine. There were lots of bare bellies showing.

Bare bellies that didn't jiggle like hers did.

"I do. I know that Daisy likes the attention, and I like talking to people about her. Uncle Tadgh sells them, so it helps whenever I show them off, so I feel like I'm helping my family. Is that so wrong?"

She knew it wasn't really a popular thing to do. She wasn't trying to strike out on her own or do anything for herself. She was just trying to help her Uncle Tadgh and be a contributing part of the family. She enjoyed it.

"No. You don't have to get all huffy about it. I wasn't insulting you. I was just teasing you."

"Oh." She closed her mouth, knowing that she did have a tendency to get a little prickly with him. But that's just because he was trying to look at Shanna over the top of her head.

"Do you want me to get out of the way so you can see her better?" she finally asked, when he wasn't saying anything.

He grinned. "She hates me. Which is fine. I don't really like her that much anyway, but she is nice to look at."

"So is my cow," Ellen said, not really meaning to insult Shanna but realizing belatedly that she probably did. Especially when Travis huffed out a laugh.

"Well, if I had to choose between the two of them—"

"I'd choose my cow," Ellen said, crossing her arms over her chest, leaning against Daisy, putting her side toward Travis.

"Well, you can choose whichever one you want. I...would probably take the cow too. It would make a lot more sense."

"Sometimes life doesn't make sense," Ellen muttered.

"You got that right."

She remembered about his mother and the trouble that he had. She wasn't sure whether he would consider it prying if she asked, but she figured she would. He could tell her to buzz off if he wanted to.

"Did your mom ever get out of jail?"

"How did you know she was locked up?"

"It's a small town."

"Yeah. She was just in for a day until she sobered up."

"She okay?"

"She's back working, if that's what you mean. We've got a huge bill to pay, because she trashed the bar with her boyfriend, or I don't even know if he was a boyfriend, and they split the bill between the two of them. I don't know where in the world we're going to come up with money for that. Maybe the sheriff will take her back to jail for it."

"Maybe that would be for the best?" Ellen asked. She said it as a statement, but she really meant it as a question.

"It might be for all that. The only problem is, not sure I would get custody of my brothers, and I don't want them to split the family apart."

"You're seventeen, aren't you?"

"Going to be eighteen soon. But sometimes courts don't have a whole lot of common sense."

"You can't work full-time until you graduate."

"You don't need to worry about it. I'll take care of my family."

"I wasn't worried. But if there's something that I can do—"

"I don't need charity. Especially from a thirteen-year-old."

"Relax. Let's talk about something else. I wasn't expecting you to get so upset."

"I'm sorry. Just a little bit...touchy on that subject. I work hard, but it seems like everything's always against me, you know?"

"Yeah. I get that."

"How could you? You have a secure home—"

"I don't have a mom or dad, in case you didn't notice, just an uncle, who is a little bit on the crazy side."

"Your uncle just got married."

"I know. And she's pretty much the best thing that's ever happened to either one of us, but I'm thirteen. For the first thirteen years of my life, I didn't have all that."

"But you have it now. So that's a good thing."

"All right. You have to admit the tables could turn on you at any time. I mean, Shanna could smile at you, and the world would be right."

She should stop talking about Shanna. Stop continuously bringing her into the conversation. Travis was going to know exactly how she felt.

"She would need to do a lot more than smile at me to make everything all right."

"I thought you didn't like her."

"I don't. I just said. I don't really want her, but I don't seem to be able to stop looking at her. Which is annoying. Because I don't want to. Because I know I'm better off with someone like you."

It would have been a great comment, except he made a fist and chucked her chin, in a playful gesture imitating something a man might do to a little kid.

She wanted to slap his hand away and tell him that she wasn't a little kid, but she knew she was only thirteen, and to a seventeen-year-old, she looked like a little kid.

The call sounded for the start of the parade, and even though Ellen knew she wouldn't be moving for a long time, since she was near the back, she straightened.

"Well, I guess it's time for me to get started."

"I can walk with you if you want me to."

She looked over at him. "Really?"

He would want to be seen with her in the parade? She could hardly believe it, but maybe it was just so he could walk behind Shanna and watch her the whole time the parade was going on.

"Sure. If you want, I'll even hold the lead rope for you."

"Well. What a help you are to this damsel in distress."

"Seriously, Ellen. You know that if you needed me, I would really help you. I mean, there haven't been too many other people who have been as nice to me as you and your uncle have, and I owe you. So, if you ever need anything, you can just ask."

"That goes both ways. If you would ever need anything, working man, just ask. I might only be thirteen, but I'm stout."

He laughed, as she figured he would, because it was true, and to her surprise, he ended up walking with her through the whole parade route. And maybe it was just her imagination, but he didn't seem to look at Shanna once.

Chapter 29

"**Y**ou and Rosie seemed to have a lot to talk about after the parade was over."

Mav sat on the porch swing, his arm around his wife, contentment seeping into his bones. He couldn't believe his life had turned out quite so perfectly.

The only dark spot was whether or not they were going to get the money, but, honestly, he didn't even care about that. As long as Cassie was with him, he was willing to go wherever he needed to go or do whatever he needed to do. Sell the ranch, move to town, or move across the country. With Cassie, he felt he could do anything because she believed in him.

She was the first person outside of his family who actually thought he was the man he wanted to be.

He wasn't, of course, but she acted like he was, like he could do anything, like she respected him and loved him and saw him as a responsible, godly man.

It made him feel like he could conquer the world. Or at least his little corner of it.

"We made a deal that I'd come over on Thursdays to help her with the Percherons. I had to talk to you, first, of course, but I told her I thought you'd be all for it."

"I am." His words were easy. "I assume I'm allowed to come, too?"

She laughed softly, the sound shimmering on the midnight air. They'd stayed to watch the fireworks, but he'd been too keyed up to sleep and had asked her to sit with him on the porch. She hadn't hesitated to say yes. He wasn't sure if that was her making herself do it or if she wanted to.

She acted like she wanted to, all snuggled up beside him. He hoped she wanted to.

"Of course. It wouldn't be any fun if you weren't there."

Her words made his heart beat hard.

"I guess I feel the same way." He wished he were better at saying the words she wanted to hear.

"You like being with yourself, too?" she teased him gently.

He smiled, his arm tightening around her.

"No, silly. Everything is more fun if you're there with me." He paused. He was going to try to tell her how he felt. But being serious and giving anyone a glimpse of the things that were important to him wasn't something he was used to doing.

He took a breath. "I...You believe in me. It makes me feel like I can do anything as long as you're with me." Like she was the part, the person, he'd been missing all his life.

She swallowed, but didn't say anything.

"I love you."

There. He said it. He held his breath.

"I guess you already know I love you, too." Her voice was soft. "And you might already know that I liked waking up beside you the night we slept on the floor."

He'd slept better on the floor that night than he'd slept in his whole life before. He'd stayed there, too, long after he woke, just so he could watch her wake in his arms. It counted as one of the best moments of his life. His wedding being at the top.

Although this moment, this beautiful, magical night where Cassie just told him she loved him...this might even top that.

His throat closed. It was one of the few times in his life where he couldn't find any words. Not even the wrong ones.

"I...I hoped we could do that again." She paused. "Tonight."

His heart gave one slow thump then seemed to stop.

Maybe she wasn't saying exactly what he hoped she was, but even if she wasn't, he'd take whatever she was offering.

"Yes," he finally choked out.

"Are you okay?" She sounded concerned and...insecure. Maybe she'd taken his inability to string two words together as disinterest? Surely not.

But, just in case, he said, "Yes. I've dreamed of you saying that, but it's hard to believe it's actually happening."

"I...I've wanted to say something for a while, but I wasn't sure how you felt." Her breath blew out slowly. "You didn't seem very interested in kissing me."

"I didn't want to push you." That was true. He'd tried to work on building a relationship, which was what she wanted and needed. He'd found he wanted it too. Wanted to know her. Wanted her to know him. Wanted to share everything with her.

"Oh." She sounded relieved, but not like she completely believed him.

"It's true. You wanted a relationship. Wanted us to get to know each other. And, I found the more I knew about you, the more I wanted to know. I wanted us to be solid. Of course, I wanted kissing too, but I thought you might mistake that for me going back on my word of allowing you to decide, or that I wasn't interested in knowing you. Because you're more than a physical relationship to me. I don't want you to not feel valued for who and what you are."

"You've made me feel cherished, just because you've been willing to give up what you want just to make me feel comfortable." The swing creaked. "And I do. Feel comfortable."

She moved against his side, pulling away just a little.

"I'm happy to hear it," he said, wishing she wasn't going to leave him.

"Mav?"

"Hmm?" he asked, wondering what he was supposed to do now. Even after what she'd said, maybe she didn't mean what he thought she meant.

"I want to move into your room."

"That's where I want you."

"Good." Her hand landed on his leg, a lot higher up than he was expecting. He managed not to jump. "Will you kiss me now?"

That was a question she didn't have to ask twice. He moved, sliding his arms around her and pulling her close, holding her like the precious treasure she was to him, and kissing her with all the emotion he hadn't been able to express in words.

It seemed to be enough.

His phone buzzed in his pocket.

Really?

He'd finally kissed his wife the way he really wanted to and someone was going to call him...after midnight?

He tore his lips away. It couldn't be good news.

Cassie seemed to have already figured that out. He could see her puckered brows in the soft moonlight.

But she didn't say anything, just watched as he pulled his phone out of his pocket glancing at the screen before swiping and putting it to his ear.

"Hello?"

"Maverick Stryker?"

The lawyer. The funny little man from the petting zoo. Mr. Czeitzler.

"Yes?" He took his arm from Cassie and pushed the speaker button so she could hear, too.

"This is Peregrine Czeitzler. You had come asking about a letter and wanting to know if it would still be good if you didn't actually have a license to get married until after the date expired."

Mav looked at his wife. His stomach clenched, then relaxed. He'd just told himself it didn't matter not that long ago. And, he was pleased to see, it really didn't. Not to him. And if the look on her face was saying what he thought it was, it didn't matter to her, either.

His eyes dropped to her lips. A little swollen, and glistening in the moonlight.

He lowered his head and kissed them. She didn't hesitate, but kissed him back. He lifted his head and met her eyes, smiling, even if they were half-closed.

That one kiss didn't feel like enough. He lowered his head and kissed her again.

"Mr. Stryker?"

The lawyer's voice brought him back to the present.

He lifted his head, but trailed his lips over his wife's temple. This phone call had to end.

"Yeah?"

"The money will be deposited into your account tomorrow at nine."

He blinked. Just like that?

His gaze sought out Cassie's. She seemed surprised, too, but she also looked like she was ready for the call to end. That made two of them.

"Sounds great. Thanks."

The man said something else, but Mav was kissing his wife again and barely managed to grunt before he swiped his phone off and dropped it somewhere, just because he needed it out of his hand in order to put both hands on either one of Cassie's cheeks, so he could cradle her head as he kissed her. Or maybe he wanted to pull her closer. She wasn't nearly close enough.

She seemed to feel the same way, because her hands pulled him tighter and she pressed closer and he was pretty sure neither one of them was thinking about money, even a billion dollars.

Chapter 30

Cassie smiled. She wanted to stretch, kind of like a satisfied cat, but she didn't want to wake her husband who snored softly beside her.

She lay on her side with her head on his arm, her leg thrown over his, her arm around his waist. She moved her hand slightly, feeling the hairy, warm skin, so different from her own.

Her lips tilted up even more. He was so much different than her. But he'd been so considerate, so careful, so sweetly gentle and tender.

She hadn't thought it would have been possible for him to make her love him anymore than she had all her life, but every day they'd been married she'd fallen deeper and tonight…she'd never felt this kind of feeling for anyone in her life before. Hadn't known that kind of deep, sweet, strong feeling was possible.

He'd charmed and disarmed her with a tender side she'd never guessed he possessed. And there was no doubt she was helplessly, hopelessly, in love with her husband.

From the way he'd cradled and kissed her, she was pretty sure he felt the same. Although she wouldn't mind if he woke up and confirmed her feelings. After all the years of dreaming, it was so hard for her to believe Mav Stryker really, truly loved her.

"You're awake?" His voice was rough. Scratchy. It gave her shivers.

"I'm sorry. I didn't mean to wake you."

"I can't believe I fell asleep. I didn't want to miss one second of the best night of my life."

"Really?" That was a good sign.

"Really. I love you doesn't feel like it says enough, but it's true. I love you."

She smiled. "You don't have to stop saying it."

"I love you." He kissed her head, his legs moving out from under hers as he turned toward her. "I'll say it as often as you want me to. I'll probably say it more often. It's something I don't want you to doubt."

She kissed his chin. "I'm not going to turn that down."

"Hmm. I wonder if there's something else you won't turn down?" His breath flowed over her temple.

"Try me."

"Kiss me."

He was right. She wasn't going to turn that down. And, unbelievably, the best night of her life managed to get even better.

Enjoy this preview of *Just a Cowboy's Love Story,* just for you!

Just a Cowboy's Love Story

Chapter 1

"I guess we're going to have to do this on our own," Sorrell said, sitting on the ground, forming a triangle with her sister and her friend making up the other corners.

"We're just kids. What are we going to be able to do?" Merritt, her sister, said, using a stick to dig in the dirt. She had gotten quite a hole dug, four inches deep or so. Which, considering it was an old, abandoned lot behind their mom's diner in Sweet Water, North Dakota, wasn't too shabby.

"Lots of times, kids can do a lot," Sorrell said, but she knew her tone wasn't very confident. She was only ten. How was she going to find a husband for her mom and a dad for herself and her sister when she was only ten?

Her friend, Toni, who was also ten, didn't seem to be paying attention to their conversation.

Her mom was also unmarried, and she hadn't even known her dad.

She didn't talk about it too much, but Sorrell was pretty sure her mom got pregnant before she graduated from high school, and the father hadn't wanted to have a kid.

Toni understood Sorrell and Merritt's predicament, even though Sorrell and Merritt had vague memories of their dad, since he and their mom had gotten divorced when they were just little.

"No wonder she likes to hang out behind the diner so much. Your mom's always burning things and sending one of us out to throw things in her pan."

"Is that what you're looking at?" Sorrell said, twisting around until she saw Munchy snorting happily at her food pan.

She hadn't even noticed. She'd been deep in thought about how they could figure out how to match their mom up.

She wanted to snap at her friend, tell her to pay attention and think of something.

But a lot of times, Toni was thinking when she didn't seem to be paying attention.

"We helped the three old men. Their video was at 1.3 million views the last I saw it. They wouldn't have had that without us," Merritt said, and she still seemed to be latched onto the idea that the three old men who took cooking classes at the diner were somehow going to help them find a man for their mom.

Sorrell had given up on that idea the second Mr. Marshall suggested Paul as a potential match. There was no way. If that was who those men thought would be a good husband for her mom, she wasn't the slightest bit interested in getting any more names from them. She'd do without a dad before she wanted a dad like that.

That didn't mean she wasn't going to help the old men.

They'd made a promise, and she had to keep her promise. The men had kept their end of the bargain, giving them a name. Just because Sorrell didn't like the name didn't mean she got out of her end of the deal.

The deal was that the men would give them a potential match for their mom, and she and her friends would help them use TikTok and set up videos that people would want to watch.

And they had. If 1.3 million views were any indication.

"Although, that video isn't really helping them, because they're not getting anyone they can talk to. They're just views and likes and some comments," Merritt said, her brows crinkled.

"I know. But it's dangerous to put your address up on social media."

That was the only video they'd made so far. The men had suggested they make one letting the ladies know where they needed to go, but Sorrell had dragged her feet at that suggestion.

Her mom had always said that social media could be dangerous, and while she wasn't sure exactly what anyone would do to hurt the old men, she did know there were some pretty crazy people in the world.

"Incoming!" Toni shouted, jumping up and scrambling to the side, grabbing Merritt's and Sorrell's hands as she did so, dragging them along with her.

Sorrell stumbled to her feet, taking big steps trying to catch her balance as Toni dragged her away.

Beside her, she could see Merritt having the same issue, and at one point, Toni pulled her through the dirt with both of her legs dragging.

Pounding hooves made it clear that Toni hadn't been exaggerating the danger, and she wouldn't be dragging Merritt over the dirt if it weren't serious.

By the time they managed to get about twenty yards from where they'd been sitting, Toni stopped and turned around.

Sorrell stopped with her and turned just in time to see Munchy storming by while Billy, the Highlander cow who roamed around Sweet Water, chased the hog just as fast as his stubby legs could go.

He wasn't a miniature, but he must have been some kind of cross, because he wasn't as big as a normal steer.

No one knew who owned either one of the animals, but the town had gotten together to make sure they had feed and water on a daily basis in the lot behind the diner.

It just so happened to be the lot that Sorrell and Merritt and Toni normally hung out in when they weren't in school.

It was kind of like their hideout, only they were in plain sight of anyone who went behind the first row of houses in town. The ones that lined Main Street.

"I don't understand why Billy is always chasing Munchy." Toni shook her head, looking over at Merritt. "I'm sorry. I knew we needed to get out of there. You know how they are when Billy gets his eye set on Munchy."

"It's okay," Merritt said, brushing off the knees of her jeans where they dragged in the dirt and were now dusty. "That's not the first time I almost got trampled. I'm glad you grabbed a hold of me and pulled. I might have gotten in their way."

"Billy's so gentle. I can't believe he'd run over you, but I think Munchy would eat you if she could." Sorrell didn't have a whole lot of time for pigs. They smelled bad.

"She's sweet. I don't know why you always have such a hard time with her," Toni said, looking after the pig. "I scratch her a lot, and she loves it. She even lies down beside me."

"I've heard pigs are really smart."

"Munchy is. But she can't seem to shake Billy."

"That makes Billy the dumb one. He doesn't seem to understand that he's not a pig," Toni pointed out

"Or he doesn't understand that Munchy isn't a cow."

"He's a steer. He shouldn't be interested in female cows anyway. Female any things."

"Well, you saw what I did, and wc all know that Billy isn't chasing her to be mean to her. He's chasing her because he likes her," Toni said, brushing off some dirt that Merritt had missed on her jeans.

Toni was almost as much of a big sister to Merritt as Sorrell was.

Sorrell knew Toni wanted little brothers and sisters of her own. Kids she could play with and take care of and mother. The way she loved to do.

Sometimes at school when Sorrell heard people complaining about their siblings, she wondered why God gave siblings to some people and didn't give them to others.

"It's too bad we can't get whatever Munchy uses to attract Billy and give it to our mom," Merritt said as she stepped back over to where they'd been sitting.

Toni laughed. "Or give it to some man who comes in the diner so your mom will actually notice a man. She's so busy working, she doesn't pay attention to anything other than her job."

"And us. She pays attention to us."

"Yeah. But that's what moms are supposed to do."

"Not all moms do."

"I know. But she doesn't get credit for paying attention to her kids. And she would get credit for paying attention to her husband, because it's extra. She needs to get her nose out of her kids and her business and start paying attention to the men around here. They're getting snatched up so fast we barely get a hold of one and somebody else has married him." Toni plopped back down on the ground, leaning back and lying down in the dirt.

But Sorrell was thinking.

Was there something to that?

She looked over at the food pan.

It was true that Munchy ate a lot of her mom's food. Could it be something in her mom's cooking?

Her mom was always looking for perfect recipes. Recipes that people loved and would come back for. Recipes that made them feel happy when they were done eating. Recipes that warmed them from the tips of their toes to the tops of their heads and made them feel content and satisfied and like eating was a pleasure.

She joked that she wanted them to have good memories of coming in the diner. And since it was kind of old and raggedy looking, the only thing she could do was to make the food so good they didn't notice how old and ugly and run down everything else looked.

Was it possible her food somehow made Munchy appealing to Billy?

That Munchy ate the food, and she no longer looked old and raggedy to Billy, but fun and happy and appealing, and Billy just wanted to be with her?

Sorrell bit her lip.

Was it possible that they could tweak one of her mom's recipes just a little? Tweak it enough that a man would eat it and her mom wouldn't be able to take her eyes off him?

Maybe it wasn't just eating it one time. Maybe they needed to find a man who would eat it every day.

She wasn't sure. Didn't know if maybe there was a special blend of ingredients that might work.

It seemed Munchy had found the secret. Or had eaten the secret. Or something.

"Hey, do you girls want to come play baseball?" Owen came around the side of the building, tossing a ball up with his right hand and catching it with the mitt that covered his left.

"They just want us because they don't have enough boys to make up the team. They wouldn't ask us if they had guys who could take our place," Toni muttered, and she didn't look inclined to want to go.

"Were we doing something else?" Sorrell asked, with her brows raised. After all, who cared why they'd askcd. It just mattered that they did.

"I like his sister. She's nice," Merritt said, standing up. "And usually they have her playing."

"Come on, Toni, don't be so prickly," Sorrell said, sitting up and bumping her friend's shoulder with her own.

"All right. But we have to keep thinking about this. There's got to be something we can do. I want a dad."

She knew she sounded a little bit demanding, but it was true. Everybody else had a dad, except for Toni, and she wanted one too. She wanted someone who would teach her how to play baseball, so when the guys asked her to play, they didn't make fun of her for throwing like a girl and not being able to hit the ball.

"You will. We're working on it. And God wouldn't want us all to grow up without a dad, so we can be sure He's going to give us one. We just have to wait until He finds the right guy." Merritt hadn't said much, and her words were soft.

"God hasn't lost anyone. He knows exactly where everyone is. He could send one any time." Sorrell didn't mean to be impatient, and she definitely didn't want to be sacrilegious, but she was of the mind that if she wanted a dad, she'd better go get one and give God a little bit of help with His job.

Maybe that wasn't quite the attitude she should have, but she kind of thought if she waited on God, she'd never get a dad.

She stood, brushing her butt off so the boys didn't make fun of her for having dirt on it, and followed her friends around the corner to the new ballpark the town had put in not long ago.

She tucked away the idea of a secret sauce, or elixir, or something, to use at some point.

Better yet, she had an idea.

"Merritt, Toni. Wait."

Toni looked a little annoyed, but she stopped and turned around with her hands on her hips. "If they start playing before we get there, they probably won't let us join."

"I won't take long. I just have an idea. When we're not busy and not playing baseball or going to school, I want you to stake out the diner." She looked at her little sister. She was cute with blue eyes and curly blonde hair, and adults were always talking about what an adorable little girl she was.

"Stake out the diner? What do you mean?"

"I mean, men come in here, they're not married, and before we can grab them for ourselves, the town matchmakers get them matched up with someone else, or someone snatches them up before we get a chance. We need to find a man, and we need to get to him before anybody else does. Got that?"

"All right," Merritt said, still looking a little unsure, but Merritt was nothing if not tenacious, and if Sorrell told her to stake out the diner, she wouldn't leave her post, even if she wasn't sure what she was supposed to be doing at that post.

"And you." She pointed to Toni. "I want you to stake out the rest of the town. Same deal. If a man comes in and he's not married, you're going to pounce on him. You call in the reinforcements—that's us—" she said, looking at Merritt and herself.

"I knew that," Toni said.

"And we'll figure out how to get him before anyone else does. Okay?"

"All right," Toni said, not sounding like she believed the plan was going to be any better than any of the other plans that they'd had, but at least it was a plan.

"What are you going to do?" Toni asked, crossing her hands over her chest and looking at Sorrell.

"I am going to search the Internet for love potions."

Pick up your copy of *Just a Cowboy's Love Story* by Jessie Gussman today!

A Gift from Jessie

Claim your free book from Jessie!

Escape to more faith-filled romance series by Jessie Gussman!

The Complete Sweet Water, North Dakota Reading Order:

Series One: Sweet Water Ranch Western Cowboy Romance (11 book series)

Series Two: Coming Home to North Dakota (12 book series)

Series Three: Flyboys of Sweet Briar Ranch in North Dakota (13 book series)

Series Four: Sweet View Ranch Western Cowboy Romance (10 book series)

Spinoffs and More! Additional Series You'll Love:

Jessie's First Series: Sweet Haven Farm (4 book series)

Small-Town Romance: The Baxter Boys (5 book series)

Bad-Boy Sweet Romance: Richmond Rebels Sweet Romance (3 book series)

Sweet Water Spinoff: Cowboy Crossing (9 book series)

Holiday Romance: Cowboy Mountain Christmas (6 book series)

Small Town Romantic Comedy: Good Grief, Idaho (5 book series)

True Stories from Jessie's Farm: Stories from Jessie Gussman's Newsletter (3 book series)

Reader-Favorite! Sweet Beach Romance: Blueberry Beach (8 book series)

Cowboy Mountain Christmas Spinoff: A Heartland Cowboy Christmas (9 book series)

Blueberry Beach Spinoff: Strawberry Sands (10 book series)